When they found her, sh[...]
with an empty bucket in [...]
her what she was called, [...]
family was, her memory was a blank. So now, the girl
has been deposited in an orphanage, where she
dresses in the same clothes as the others, and attends
the same lessons, but even here, she and they know
that she doesn't quite fit. Somewhere, within the girl's
sturdy, slow body, beneath her watchful silence, the
truth about her identity and her past lies hidden, until –
in spare, harsh prose – Erpenbeck draws it coolly out.

The Old Child

JENNY ERPENBECK was born in East Berlin in 1967. She learned bookbinding, studied theatre sciences and worked backstage at the Staatsoper theatre in Berlin before becoming an opera director and writer. She has now published a play and a collection of short stories. Her fiction has been translated worldwide and *The Old Child* was awarded one of Germany's Aspekte Prizes for Literature. This year she has been manning Germany's most charming literary post, as Poet of the Island of Sylt.

SUSAN BERNOFSKY has translated works by Robert Walser, Hermann Hesse, Gregor von Rezzori, Yoko Tawada, Ludwig Harig and Peter Szondi. She is the author of *Foreign Words: Translator-Authors in the Age of Goethe* and is currently at work on a biography of Robert Walser. Her translation of *The Old Child and Other Stories* was awarded the Helen and Kurt Wolff Prize 2006.

The Old Child

Jenny Erpenbeck

*Translated from the German
by Susan Bernofsky*

BOOKS

Published by Portobello Books Ltd 2006

Portobello Books Ltd
Eardley House
4 Uxbridge Street
Notting Hill Gate
London W8 7SY, UK

Copyright © Jenny Erpenbeck 1999

Translation © Susan Bernofsky 2005

First published in the original German by Eichborn
Verlag AG Frankfurt am Main as *Geschichte vom alten Kind*
in 1999. First published in English simultaneously by New
Directions in the USA and by Penguin Books Canada
in *The Old Child & Other Stories* in 2005.

A CIP catalogue record is available from the British Library

2   4   6   8   9   7   5   3   1

ISBN 1 84627 056 1

13-digit ISBN 978 1 84627 056 7

www.portobellobooks.com

Designed and typeset in Poliphilus
by Patty Rennie Production, Portsoy

Printed in Great Britain

For my mother

When they found her, she was standing on the street with an empty bucket in one hand, on a street lined with shops, and didn't say a word. When she was brought to the police station, all the official questions were put to her: What her name was, where she lived, her parents, her age. The girl replied that she was fourteen years old, but she couldn't tell them her name, nor where her home was. At first, the policemen had called the girl "miss", but now they stopped. They said: How can you not know where you came from, where you were before you stood on the street here with your empty bucket? The girl simply could not remember, she couldn't remember the beginning. She was an orphan through and through, and all she had, all she knew was the empty bucket she held in one hand and continued to hold as the policemen questioned her. One of the men tried to insult the girl, saying: Scraping the bottom of the bucket, eh? But the girl didn't even notice that his words were meant to give offense, she replied simply: Yes.

The official inquiries produced no further information. The girl was indisputably present in all her height and bulk, but as for her origins and history, she was so surrounded by nothingness that there seemed, from the beginning, to be something implausible about her very existence. So they relieved her of her bucket, took her by her fleshy hand, and brought her to the Home for Children.

The girl has a wide, blotchy face that looks like a moon with shadows on it, she has broad shoulders like a swimmer's, and from the shoulders downward she appears to have been hewn from a single block of wood, there is neither a swelling where the breasts should be, nor an indentation at the waist. The legs are sturdy, the hands as well, and nonetheless the girl does not make a convincing impression, perhaps because of her hair. This hair is neither long nor short, it forms a fringe at the nape of the neck and is neither brown nor genuinely black—it is at most as black as the cloth of a flag that has been hanging too long in the sun and is bleached out, there are moments when it appears nearly gray. The girl moves slowly, and if she should happen not to move slowly, little beads of sweat appear on the bridge of her nose. The girl knows she is bigger than she should be, and so she hunches her shoulders and keeps her head down. She hunches as though she were obliged to do so, to hold back a great force that is raging inside her.

The home where the police have deposited the girl is the largest in this city. It is located in the city's most outlying district, the district that borders the woods, and is comprised of several buildings distributed across the extensive, meandering grounds. There are living quarters, a nursery school, a school for the lower and one for the upper classes, as well as a kitchen building, a gymnasium, an assembly hall, a quadrangle paved in concrete, a soccer field, and outbuildings in which various workshops are housed—here the pupils are to learn to work hard, just as Life will one day require of them. Surrounding all this there is a fence, a fence with a single gate at which a guard is posted, one has to speak with him to enter the Home or leave it. Through this gate, the down-at-heels or prosperous parents come to visit on weekends, weeping parents and parents who do not weep, but for some of the children, neither down-at-heels, nor prosperous, nor weeping, nor any other sort of parents pass through this gate. The gate also admits strangers who wish to become parents, they come here to have a look at the children, but for some children even strangers do not come. There are children that are so unclean, so massive or coarse that they need not even be rejected: no one looks at them to begin with, they cannot pass through the screen that has been woven to aid in these selections. They are here, but no one sees them. The girl will doubtless be one of these. And yet her invisibility appears to be something even more fundamental: the entire figure of the girl is so askew—even her way of walking is askew—that if you wanted to take her by the hand it would be like thrusting your hand into emptiness.

On this still-warm day in autumn, then, the girl can walk across the thin grass of the sports field without the least agitation, despite all the parents, or those who wish to become parents, seated on the wooden rails that frame the field. For while these parents and would-be parents keep their eyes fixed on the field, observing their children, or the children who will one day be theirs, engaged in various activities, they do not take note of the girl, it is as if she were impervious to their glances. None of these down-at-heels and weeping and other sorts of parents, nor any of the strangers who wish to become parents will see her walking across the field. That's just the way she's planned it. Just as others strive to break out of fenced-in enclosures, to escape from prison, the workhouse, the insane asylum or barracks, the girl has achieved quite the opposite: she has broken into such an enclosure, the Home for Children to be precise, and it is highly unlikely that anyone would think of taking her back out through the gate, thrusting her back into the world.

And so she walks across the field with utter calm, gnawing as she goes upon her fingernail. And when on her very first day one of the littlest boys bumps into her as she is walking across the field with her nail between her lips, bumps her so that she almost falls down and has to catch herself with one hand, she begins to sob for one brief moment, but this she finds not unpleasurable. For the circumstance that a little boy has bumped her to make her fall in the mud, indeed has bumped her so hard she has to sob, awakens in the girl the hope that she will be permitted to occupy one of the lower rungs in the school's hierarchy, perhaps even the lowermost one, and the lowermost place is always the safest, it is the one whose requirements she will most definitely be able to live up to. And so she doesn't even wipe the mud from her hand, but instead continues to walk, still sobbing just a little, and then goes back to gnawing her fingernail, which now is dirty.

When they first brought her to her room, which is above all a room for sleeping, to be shared with three other girls, it was one of the happiest moments of her life. This room was free of disorder of any sort, it contained four beds, each placed against one of the four walls, and all four of them neatly made up, and beside each one a chair and a metal locker. The locker is meant to hold the week's bundle of clothes, as well as the books for school and notebooks, and the few personal items a child might collect or, if it has saved enough, buy with its pocket money. To be sure, the economical child is as likely as not to find these items stolen. As a matter of principle, the lockers have no locks. A communal spirit is to be fostered. All the items a child brings with it when it enters the Home are confiscated and then discarded, for its arrival here constitutes a New Beginning.

At this time of day, none of the other girls is in the room, because it is not yet bedtime and entering the room before bedtime is not permitted. It isn't a room for daytime activities. The instructress speaks, the girl listens and nods, she is allowed to peer briefly into her locker, in which everything is already arranged just as will be expected from now on. For a moment she thinks of her bucket, which always made a sound like someone sighing when it swung back and forth. Then she is told to take off everything she is wearing. She sits down on the edge of the bed and begins to pull off her trousers, then the stockings she is wearing beneath them, of good quality but full of holes, and she crosses her arms above her head to free herself from her matted woolen sweater, which is much too tight. Just imagine, she crosses her arms above her head for this, like a woman. The girl undresses down to a grayish camisole and grayish panties, then she gets up and trots after the instructress, who has gestured for her to follow. The instructress walks across the linoleum of the windowless hallway to the washroom, the girl behind her. In the washroom she then surrenders her camisole and steps out of her panties, balancing on one leg at a time, ducking her head and glancing up at the instructress who is standing beside her, observing this obligatory transformation. The instructress has placed the girl's other things over her arm, and to these she now adds the camisole and panties. Now that she is naked, the girl looks very much like a block of wood. She gets up and steps into the shower. She begins to wash herself. Finally she is able to wash off the dirt covering her entire body, dirt such as collects on a body over time.

After the girl has washed, the instructress gives her the packet of clothes for the week. This clothing is issued by the laundry staff, all of the things are second, third and fourth hand, but they have been washed and are the right size for the recipient of the package. The girl slips into this clothing that has been assigned to her. While a number will be sewn into the sweaters, pants and skirts indicating that they will now belong to the girl until she outgrows them, the underpants and undershirts as well as the nightgowns count as "linens", which means that once a week each child receives one pair of underpants, one undershirt and one nightgown as part of the general laundry distribution, the underwear is, as it were, intended to clothe a single collective body, and anyone who is unhappy with this arrangement will be addressed as madame, and her protest will bear no fruit. But there is no need to address the girl as madame, she finds nothing to object to in this procedure and is moreover familiar with the charming admonition

"No false delicacy!" of which this laundry arrangement reminds her. In any case, the collective underpants restore to order something that had been threatened by disorder, that's what it feels like to the girl.

When she has then attained this condition, clad in the same standard-issue clothes as all the others here, and clean to precisely the same extent as all the others, she goes looking for a mirror. She wants to see what she looks like in this new life of hers, wants to see whether her face has changed with the advent of this New Life, but as she discovers, her new room has no mirror. She will wander about and notice that neither in the bathrooms nor in any of the halls, nor anywhere else in the Home has a mirror been provided. Finally she will ask, already anticipating the first twinges of a guilty conscience, and therefore as casually as possible, whether there is a mirror, and she will learn that vanity is one of the seven deadly sins, madame. And while the reproach contained in this answer demonstrates that the instructress is utterly blind to the nature of the causes that lead the girl to look for a mirror and, indeed, to eventually ask for one, her response illumines the principle that governs this fenced-in institution, and the girl knows no happier state than what she experiences when gazing upon the architecture of a principle. She knows no brighter, more beautiful sight.

The girl remembers the time of mirrors, when she noticed, at first with unease, then with interest and finally with satisfaction, indeed even a sort of pride, that her face had looked utterly unchanged for quite a long time, as if its round, fleshy form were repelling age. The girl had then begun to experiment with this unchangingness. For example, when an occasion for weeping presented itself, she would take advantage of this occasion to weep profusely and when she was done weeping would quickly go look at herself in the mirror. And behold, neither had her cheeks gone hollow with the exertion of her weeping, nor had her skin become porous, nor had shadows come to encircle her eyes. So she could weep as much as she liked and nonetheless be quite certain that this weeping would leave no traces behind on her large face. Another time, she lied to someone and checked in a mirror to see whether her face had been transformed into the face of a liar, but either her face had been from the beginning a liar's face or it simply had not changed as a result of the lie, though before the lie it hadn't been a liar's face and afterward, while it remained the same, it was the face of a liar. Even the time someone had unexpectedly given her a very beautiful leather wallet stamped with the Leaning Tower of Pisa, she looked in the mirror, but the pleasure could not be distinguished in her features. Observing the constancy of her face, which is what made the girl acquire the habit of frequently looking in the mirror, hardly counts as vanity, but now the view that vanity was one of the seven deadly sins had been invoked to justify why it was not possible to view one's own reflection anywhere in the Home, and the girl noted with gratitude that to her, as to all the others, one and the same set of reasons was being applied for encouraging one thing and discouraging another. Liberated from the task of monitoring her face, indeed forgetting it outright, the girl steps into the bright architecture of the principle upon which she has briefly been permitted to gaze.

When she came into the classroom and all the others were standing beside their desks and she herself was standing beside the teacher in front of them, she felt like Gulliver among the Lilliputians. She looked around her and saw that she could look down at all the other heads. That's when she realized she was too tall. She hunched her shoulders and waited for the teacher to assign her a seat. The teacher placed her in the one unoccupied seat, next to a boy with a rough-hewn face. That way the contrast wasn't so great, and the others were able to recover from their alarm and begin to believe that this was the new girl. The girls saw at a glance that the new girl was not a beauty who might disrupt their fine-spun hierarchy—for the moment such ponderous creatures sit down, they at once sink, a leaden sediment, to the depths of every hierarchy—and the boys knew they had landed a fine catch, sustenance for many a good laugh had just strolled right into their mouths, and this filled them with glee. From the smiling silence on the part of her classmates after she's been assigned her seat, the girl ventures to conclude that her awkwardness apparently suffices to secure her a place in this eighth-grade class, perhaps even the lowermost one, and at this she is relieved. At just this moment, a door can be heard shutting faintly somewhere, and it seems to the girl as if her old life has now departed from her.

The lesson proceeds, but the girl sits in silence, and the leaden script imprinted on her brain now tumbles into the blue sky outside the classroom windows, she surrenders each of her words and each of her thoughts until in the end she is left sitting there in a state of perfect emptiness, and one might well be moved to say of her: She is a blank slate.

This overgrown child begins to follow lessons, for example an eighth-grade lesson in mathematics: If x equals y, the straight line rises at a forty-five-degree angle. The girl listens to what is being said and to what is being thought, she listens to everything that is said and thought during an eighth-grade mathematics lesson. Somewhere she has already made the acquaintance of this straight line rising at its angle of forty-five degrees, and nonetheless she is astonished to meet it again on this side of the diagram.

Something or other must be reversed, like a mirror image, or must once have been so. It seems to the girl as if she must have switched sides at some point, but when this was she cannot say. Headfirst through the looking glass.

The girl picks up her pen and awaits the arrival of the text. She doesn't have to wait long. The letters bend mutely to the left as if encountering some invisible resistance, the "n"s rehoist their flattened hillocks, the double underlines, executed with the aid of a ruler, present themselves content‐edly for inspection. A lost age makes its entrance on a carpet of blue ink. The teacher picks up the notebook by the ears and says: Now you've got it.

On this side of the diagram it is customary to raise one's hand when one has something to say. One may then be permitted to speak, at the teacher's discretion. The mathe‐matics teacher wants to go easy on the girl during the first lesson, to give her time to adjust, but when near the end of the hour her thick arm slowly rises above her head, he gives her a sign permitting her to speak. For the first time the girl speaks in her new circle of companions, she gives the answer to a simple question the teacher has asked, and her answer is wrong. Never mind, the teacher says, and gives the girl a particularly warm smile, since she has dared to speak for the first time, with so soft, thin and sweet a voice, a little sister of a voice, one that seems made for giving the wrong answer in the most pitiful way. That she meant to give the wrong answer, however, that she more or less stole it from her classmates, is a possibility that occurs to no one, all that can be sensed is a certain fakeness to her way of speaking, but since everyone steals in class as best he can, since everyone's eyes are directed deceptively and with faked attentiveness toward the front of the room, toward the teacher, this girlish little voice is received with a grin, and the lesson proceeds.

There must have been a time when the girl, too, thought of a bad grade as something bad, but this time is long past. Meanwhile she has learned that school is the place where errors must occur so as to give it meaning, school is the place of correction, and no bad grade has any real conse⁄

quences, grades are utterly removed from reality, they stand for the contents of a head, something invisible. And when the teachers then insist that learning is something one does not for school but for Life, this serves only to reinforce the girl's faith that school and Life are two separate things. All that can happen to her here if such occurrences become too frequent is that the teacher will eventually give up on her, he will be unable to help noticing that the girl's capacity to forget is greater than her capacity to store in her head the subject matter of an eighth-grade class—mathematics, for instance—which would allow her and her head to advance to a ninth-grade classroom at the appointed time. And while the prospect of not being allowed to pass to the next grade might fill the others with terror, implying as it does an additional year of captivity, for the girl it would be a coup. Just as she gives the subject matter its freedom back by forgetting it, she, too, would like to gain her freedom by having the teachers say: This one you can forget about. What a blessing it must be to be given up on. What a blessing to gaze upon the backs of one's fellow students who are working their way forward amid the sweat and cold because for them, whether they like it or not, school and Life appear to form a single continuum. What a blessing to be able to observe their toils with a peace-filled heart. And while it would appear to be actual stupidity, stupidity almost even greater than that of a pupil occupying the lowermost rung in the hierarchy, that accounts for the girl's having been given up on by teachers and pupils alike—for clearly she is neither lazy, nor does she refuse to perform out of ill will, nor does she think she is better than the others, no, she is simply stupid—even having been given up on is not enough to sever her sense of belonging among the others, who unlike her are expending great effort to drive their minds along in front of them. Even the pace at which she walks causes the others' successes to stand out in their full significance, and it isn't out of laziness or ill will that she walks so far behind them, nor because she thinks she is better than they are, but rather for the simple reason that she can go no faster, for, the moment she takes as many as three steps, beads of sweat appear on the bridge of her nose, indicating that she has reached her limit. And precisely because she has been given up on, and because the girl gives no one cause for envy or a struggle, you can laugh at her, you can even shove her so that she nearly falls down, for no other reason than the delight you feel at the way the girl's very presence demonstrates the antithesis between those who get somewhere in life and this girl who is simply too stupid to get anywhere. And since the girl herself is equally grateful for this antithesis, or even more so, just from a different perspective, she feels at the moment when she is being given a shove that nearly makes her fall down, a moment when she might perhaps even sob a little, a great sense of relief at occupying this lowermost place that no one will fight her for, a place that does not require extreme expenditures of effort to attain and hold, all that is needed is a meticulous forgetfulness and the meticulous stupidity that results from it, as well as letting herself be shoved and sobbing a little. While the others no doubt know what is owed to them by Life: Life owes them freedom, and freedom lies outside the walls of this institution, the girl knows that in truth freedom is this: Not having to shove anyone yourself, and this freedom exists inside the walls of the institution and nowhere else. And if she simply allows herself to be shoved, she will keep her place in the institution forever and will never have to get anywhere, not even ninth grade.

For example it may happen that the girl is sitting in German class and the teacher is asking the children about *Puntila*, which they were to have read, the play *Puntila and His Man Matti*, by Bertolt Brecht. The teacher is a young woman with bleached-blond hair, about whom the rumor is circulating among the students that after school she frequents the tin shacks of the construction workers. Now and again she mentions a gentleman acquaintance, and now and again she appears in class in the morning with red eyes. Chronic conjunctivitis, she says. Now she has asked the children about *Puntila*, whereupon the girl sits as quietly as possible in her seat and keeps her head down. Someone else would either say: Sure, I've read it, that Puntila play, and I know who Bertolt Brecht is. Then the teacher would ask some more specific questions, and probably the one who had spoken would turn out to have been lying, it would become apparent that he knew nothing at all, neither about *Puntila* nor Bertolt Brecht, and only said so to make the teacher think he was an industrious student, which in any case would mean he was resourceful—or else he would say: No, it's true, I don't know *Puntila*, and I don't know who Bertolt Brecht is, either. This would be sheer insolence, and it would mean that the one who had spoken was not timid, in other words that he was lazy but at least courageous, and this, too, would stand him in good stead, at least among his peers. Of course it isn't possible for all the children to be either resourceful or courageous, and there are several who also sit there quietly and keep their heads down, but they cannot possibly sit there just as quietly and keep their heads quite as far down as the girl, because these others, when they are quiet and keep their heads down, do so in the hope of making the teacher overlook their existence so that she will not call on them. The girl, on the other hand, when she sits there so very quietly with her head down is in fact trying to achieve precisely this: being called on by the teacher, being asked why she is sitting there so quietly, whether it is really true that she knows nothing, absolutely nothing at all about *Puntila* or Bertolt Brecht. She is all but forcing the teacher to call on her, her submissive posture produces a sort of suction that attracts the ill will of others, including the teacher. The teacher will have no choice but to ask the girl about *Puntila* and Brecht, although it is plain to see that there is not a single person anywhere in the world likely to know less about *Puntila* and Bertolt Brecht than this lumpy girl seated at this desk. Precisely for this reason she will ask her, so as to embarrass her. She will compel the girl to admit her guilt, choking with shame: It is true, I don't know anything, neither about *Puntila* nor about Bertolt Brecht. And in this way the girl will cause the teacher in her turn to feel ashamed, for having allowed herself to get carried away to the point of harassing the girl thus. The teacher, of course, has no idea that the girl herself has used suction to all but compel her to act as she has. And therefore, while any other student would be punished for this lack of knowledge, the girl will not be punished. The teacher, attempting to justify this leniency to herself, will tell herself that the girl is so fundamentally incapable of knowing anything at all that no punishment can alter her incapacity, that the girl is an absolutely lost cause and that the most fitting thing can only be to give up on her.

I am the weakest. None of these foundlings is weaker than I am.

The girl is terribly clumsy. She cannot even walk properly. While she is attempting to cross the schoolyard, she knocks into children who are playing ball or chatting in little groups—one of the smallest boys grins at her and asks: Are you the new teacher?, belches in her face and scoots off. The girl flees into a side entrance of the school building and has leapt up three wooden steps when she stops short, as if she'd come to a wall: There on the landing a couple is kissing, a tangle of hair and hands and trousers. Suddenly she is unable to see, she looks but sees nothing, it is not only the couple she cannot see, she sees nothing at all, not the stair-well, not the wooden steps, nothing in front of her and nothing behind, nothing. She opens her eyes as wide as she can, but she sees nothing.

The girl doesn't know what word to put in the blank. In her English book there are blanks marked with ellipses, and these blanks are to be filled in with a verb in the correct tense, but the girl doesn't know the correct tense. So she raises her hand. It is the teacher's duty to come over to the girl's desk, bend down and explain the method to her. The girl says Yes and nods, says Oh, I see, and with her eyes follows the teacher's thick, hairy index finger as it moves across the paper. And the moment the teacher has stood up again and turned his back on the girl with an encouraging nod, she will raise her hand again, and she can count on the teacher's once again coming to stand beside her desk, bending down and giving his explanation as he moves his index finger across the paper—he is paid for his patience. To be sure, there are instances when a pupil's stupidity might appear to be a ruse, instilling in the teacher a certain nervousness, a secret irritation which will cost him some effort to keep in check, or if it is not irritation, then it is perhaps doubt that may assail the teacher—doubt as to whether he has chosen the right profession—upon his finding a pupil's head to be as heavy as lead, incapable of absorbing the principles of rational thought. Yet it is neither nervousness, nor irritation, nor self-doubt that assails the teacher when he sees the girl holding up her hand. No, fear and pity make this English teacher tremble as he awaits the girl's signal, and each time her fleshy arm rises above her head, he will betake himself wearily to her side and with the utmost patience, often even with tears in his eyes, will repeat explanations he has already given hundreds of times over one more hopeless time, moving his hairy index finger across the blanks with their ellipses, speaking slowly, ever so slowly, in English, a language the girl will never, ever understand, even when it is spoken ever so slowly. In the teachers' lounge, his impression was confirmed by his colleagues: The girl's incapacity really did extend to all her subjects to the same degree, it was as credible as it was irre-mediable. She was cutting off her nose to spite her face, the German teacher remarked. The chronically paltry state of the girl's knowledge fills the English teacher with shame, even the sort of guilt that might be felt by a person who enjoys advantages that were attained by some subterfuge and are thus inaccessible to others. He sees himself as a sort of victor *malgré soi* in what is for the girl a hopeless contest. Thus he fails to understand the power of this raised female arm to compel, fails to understand that not only does he respond to her call, he has to respond to it, he is being torn apart—in other words, governed—by the perfectly legitimate expectation that he provide help where it is needed, coupled with his inability to provide it. Thus afflicted with blindness, he will seek to cover up his supposed guilt by addressing the German teacher forcefully on some other occasion: That girl there, he will say, a dead loss.

And so while these and other teachers quickly fall prey to the girl's well-calculated stupidity, because they are looking down at this eighth-grade classroom at such a remove of years they might as well be surveying it from on high, the situation at ground level, that is, seen from the equally valid vantage point of her fellow students, presents itself quite differently. Not that these peers of hers would be any less likely to use an answer cribbed from the lips of others to neutralize a teacher—but outside the classroom, matters appear in a different light. Just as a herd becomes restless when the One of the Cleft Foot enters its midst, these fourteen-year-olds can scent deception the moment it is directed toward them. And while the girl has no trouble making the grown-ups see of her only what she wishes them to see, no more and no less, among those her own age she displays true insecurity, and this provokes them. The girl's massive body only increases the insecurity that makes her tremble, this body practically towers above the horizon, it appears shakier than the other fourteen-year-old bodies, this shakiness is apparent to the others and is felt by them as a provocation.

Around me, everything is awhirl. No one looks at me, I don't know what I have done. These beautiful children with their childish skin, their childish teeth, their thin little bracelets—they slam the gate shut in my face. Why does no one speak to me?

The hoarse voices of adolescent boys crowd in on the girl, whose plumpness was acquired in a place she refuses to name, they ask her: Where were you? Where were you before? And the girl begins to stab at them with a pair of scissors. She stabs only air with her scissors, as the boys are quicker than she is. At the front of the room, a lesson is in progress, while in back the battle rages. Two boys grab the girl by her arms. Desperately she struggles. A third boy tries to put his hand up her skirt. The girl flails about. Shrilly the recess bell sounds. The girl tears herself loose, the boys charge off, the room empties. The girl remains alone, the scissors still in her hand, and smoothes her skirt down. She packs up her school things and leaves.

The girl is in search of something, she is trying to speak, but while the vocabulary itself appears to have nothing wrong with it, there is always a black, gaping nothingness that can be glimpsed through it, as through filigree. Everything that comes out of her mouth always looks like a lie, even if it isn't one, the girl is always giving her peers the impression that even she cannot believe herself, not even when she is speaking a truth, and then this truth ceases to be true. And when the matter at hand is too trifling for it to be a question of trust or distrust, then the ones to whom the girl has addressed herself will be overcome with boredom, and this boredom, too, originates primarily in the circum/ stance that even the girl appears bored by what she is saying, more bored than anyone else, as if everything filtered through her person is either sullied or exhausted in the process. It then reappears as a sullied or exhausted entity, and gives quite a different impression than before. As in a chemical reaction, the girl adds to every thought that passes through her head something like an invisible substance which changes the sign preceding it from positive to negative. The sentence that is the thought remains just as it was, and yet the moment the girl utters this sentence, a thought that was perfectly sincere becomes mendacious, and an interesting one descends into tedium. And so most of what the girl says founders almost at once, it drags itself by the hair into the bog no sooner than it appears, no one is obliged to find it credible, not even the girl herself, and this is most painful of all. The girl's sentences lie in her stomach like a heap of scrap metal, they cannot take root inside her, and sometimes she even looks down to see whether one of these sentences isn't poking out of her side.

The geography teacher is slimy, the others declare. In the girl's head, at the spot which in the others is occupied by an

opinion of this sort, there is only emptiness. Nonetheless she
will undertake the experiment with all the good will in the
world, and the moment she catches sight of the geography
teacher while she is shuffling down the hallway with all the
others, although she realizes that in the spot which in others
is occupied by an opinion she has only emptiness, she will
venture a comment: Everywhere he goes, she will say, that
geography teacher leaves a trail of slime behind him. All
the girl wants to do is say what any of the other pupils
would have said at just this moment, she wants to contribute
to the cohesiveness of this group which she is a part of, but
then of course even this modest undertaking proves too
much for her. Her sweet little voice fails her the moment she
begins to speak, it balks, leaves her in the lurch, presenting
itself as a cracking falsetto. Not even a voice can manage to
put down roots in this body, which, misleadingly, makes
a solid impression. The others, repelled by the inferior
manner in which the girl is parroting this view of theirs,
will understandably start looking for a new one to replace
it with.

The school dreams are returning. Dreams of changing rooms, flooded mass toilets, swimming pools with someone's hair floating into my mouth. Doors being thrust open, slammed shut, suddenly I realize that someone is watching me, someone is peering over one of the flimsy walls that go only halfway up while my piss hits the ground beside the toilet. The colors: mint green and white.

Then the girl, maintaining an appropriate distance from her classmates but mimicking their postures, squats with her back to the wall on the floor outside a classroom, awaiting the arrival of the chemistry teacher. At the moment, her inferiority is the only existing link between her and the others: that she is inadequate and is made to feel this inadequacy quite clearly, but without being able to understand in what this inadequacy consists, that she is guilty and acknowledges this guilt, but without recognizing in what it consists, that she arrives too late and apologizes, but never learns what she has arrived too late for, all these things comprise her relationship to them. When she arrives somewhere, the others are just leaving, and wherever she is, the past is about to begin, the others leave her behind for their own amusement, but she keeps tagging along behind them, like an echo.

The chemistry teacher arrives and unlocks the door to the laboratory. The mob streams in, the girl taking her place next to the boy with the rough-hewn face. The chemistry teacher stations himself behind his lab bench and begins agitating test tubes, combining their contents, holding them up in the air, and describing all that is taking place. He dissolves sodium carbonate in water and, by adding a few drops of phenolphthalein, causes this formerly clear fluid to turn purple before the astonished eyes of the fourteen-year-olds. Now he will ask: Where did the purple come from?, but no one will know the answer, there will be various whisperings and giggles, and one pupil will attempt to frighten the chemistry teacher by licking the top of his possibly contaminated desk. The girl's face throughout this class session displays contentment, for all that is being asked of her is to watch someone dissolving sodium carbonate in water and adding a few drops of phenolphthalein to produce a purple coloration, and then someone licking his possibly contaminated desktop, there are no consequences to any of this, and soon class is over and everyone leaves, everyone and the girl.

The others are walking, and as they walk they speak among themselves; the girl listens. One girl says to another: Are you going to lunch after? And the other responds to the first: If I have to look at that slop one more time... I could puke just thinking about it. The girl slows her steps, allows herself to fall behind, and further back addresses a class-mate, saying to her casually: I'm not going to lunch after, I can't stand to look at that slop, it's enough to make you puke. But the girl she has addressed doesn't say: Me too, or: Oh, I don't think the food is all that bad, or: I have to go to lunch even though it's disgusting, I'm really starving. She doesn't say any of these things, but just stares at the girl, gives a quick grimace and walks away. The girl's face is hot, as if she were suddenly terrified, she glances down at herself and, sure enough, there is the sentence she has stolen from her classmate poking out of her side.

The girl finds her way to the kitchen. She has discovered that if she loiters long enough there on her big feet, she will sometimes be given leftovers to eat when all the shifts of classes have finished their meals and some food still remains. Sometimes she has to work for this treat: She might, say, be asked to roll the empty barrels outside for pickup, and although this immediately makes her break out in a sweat, she is glad to do it, she likes the crunching sound the barrels make outside on the sand. Then she is allowed to return to the kitchen and stands in a corner to spoon up her reward. As she eats, she gazes at a stained notice that has been affixed to the tiles, this notice contains the Health Department guidelines.

No pain, no gain, the gym teacher admonishes the class at the end of every session, right when they finish their endurance training. This admonition is familiar to the girl, only she can't think from where, clearly it is something someone once imparted to her as a golden rule for life. The girl loves gym class, she thinks it's pretty when all the pupils are dressed uniformly in red and white, teams are chosen, and these teams exist for the purpose of developing team spirit. The girl possesses a great deal of team spirit, but unfortunately her body does not reflect it. On the balance beam, she lumbers about like a pale lump of dough with a head. The teacher has to force herself to look up at her. She cannot help but marvel at this creature. The creature is performing a languorous dance upon the balance beam. The primordial transition from water to land. Or else the girl runs and runs and runs, and at the end of this long race she is as pale as a sheet of paper. She isn't sure whether she will have to collapse right away, or whether she can put off this collapse until the teacher has said: Next!, she does her best to remain standing so as not to disgrace her team, but in the end when she cannot hold out any longer and measures her length in the wet grass, the teacher says the thing about pain and gain. After several gym classes, the girl realizes to her distress that merely summoning up the good will she brings to her team is already such a drain on her resources that a definite decrease in strength can be noted. This good will appears to stand in a precisely inverse proportion to what can be achieved by it. This good will is hung about one like chains and impedes all forward motion. The girl has the good will, indeed the best will, not to disgrace her team, but nonetheless she becomes slower from week to week. Maybe what she needs is a fortissimo, she tells herself, maybe she's just been running too softly.

On her way back outside, her gym bag trailing along on the ground behind her, the girl stops and stands inside the entryway to the gymnasium where the fire safety code is posted. She studies the fire safety code, and this allows her to forget her exhaustion—after every gym class she studies the fire safety code, and this makes her calm again. Meanwhile her classmates are filing outside behind her back, many of them are slurping milk out of milk cartons, because gym class has made them thirsty, they chatter, gossip and laugh, their voices vanish through the glass door, a cold draft breezes through the entryway, and the girl tries to recall the names that go with these voices, but she isn't yet able to do so. She doesn't know her classmates well enough, she cannot yet remember their names.

While she is helping the kitchen staff dry the last of the plates, the girl hears someone doing something out in the dining hall, she sticks her head through the hatch which, only an hour ago, was being used to dish out food, and sees the custodian hanging up a large map of the world, he is hanging it up back to front, with the blank side facing forward. Meanwhile a second man, one the girl doesn't know, is moving the chairs and tables around, and then the two of them together lift a large piece of apparatus onto one of the tables. Finally the custodian climbs up on a ladder and drapes a large black cloth over the windows, the other man helping. While he is climbing down, the custodian notices the girl watching him through the hatch. He says: Careful, don't stick your neck out too far, the window might fall down and chop your head off. He's expecting this to make the girl laugh. His expectations are not met. Pointing to the apparatus, he says: That's for the movie. Today is movie day. Then he goes out into the hall to unlock the glass door. A large number of children come in, they have been waiting outside, all the children are coming, including all the girl's classmates, all of them knew that today was movie day, all of them except the girl, since no one told her. The girl abandons her plate and comes from behind the hatch. She looks to see where there is still room, spies a table off to one side that already has two children sitting on it, and shuffles over to it without lifting her head, in a transport of happiness she hops onto the table, which isn't so easy. Then everything goes dark, and the show begins. First, an old wooden cottage appears on the screen, then one of its shutters is shoved open from the inside, and an old peasant woman leans out of the window and starts telling a fairy tale. Now cottage and peasant woman dissolve, and the story proper begins. It is a very sad story, and the girl begins to cry, she cannot help it, but she weeps softly so as not to disturb the others, tears drip from her chin down onto her plump hands, which she is holding clasped in her lap. She gazes and gazes, and only after quite some time has passed does she realize that the others are laughing at precisely those bits that make her cry, a few of them aren't even looking at the screen at all, but instead are pushing and shoving one another about in the best of spirits. Now the girl stops crying and carefully observes all that is happening there in the dark, then she wipes the tears from her chin as inconspicuously as possible and begins to swing her legs gently to and fro. The wooden cottage has just reappeared on the screen, this time as seen from within, and one can observe a battle in progress. Several men are attempting to drive the peasant woman from her house, but she fights back, shouting again and again: Over my dead body! Over my dead body! Hereupon one of the men draws his gun and shoots her. Now they are carrying the dead woman out of the house on a bier, and the ownership of the cottage passes to the men. The connection between this scene and the fairy tale itself is lost on the girl, but she finds it all terribly funny. She tries to show her teeth when she laughs, like the others, but laughter itself, the sound of laughter, is no longer familiar to her. The little boy sitting next to the girl notices the hoarse raspy sounds she is making, so she falls silent.

Meanwhile the girl's number has been sewn into all her clothes, her number is 9912. The child who arrived at the Home just before her has the number 9911, and there is some other one, one who arrived after, who has the number 9913, this is a perfectly ordinary series. The girl adapts to the various procedures that determine the course of life in the Home, but above all her inward submission is flawless, she practically obeys commands before they are issued. While all the other adolescents have a greater or lesser degree of talent in following instructions, with the girl it seems not to be a matter of following at all, rather it is as if she herself knows what an asset such discipline is. Should, for instance, the instructress performing the weekly inspection happen to snatch all the clothing out of a locker and throw it on the floor because it was not stacked neatly enough, this will never be clothing belonging to the girl. And when the instructress then pulls the delinquent over to her by the hair, whispering: All of my pupils are dear to me, all of them except you! this will surely not be the girl's hair. In such cases the girl will be found standing before her locker in which all the clothing is neatly stacked, observing these events out of the corner of one eye.

To the other pupils, this infallibility seems a form of betrayal, because there is something slavish about it, and because among slaves nothing is deadlier than for one of their number to voluntarily assume the slave's role. But while the girl's desire for order happens to correspond to the standards imposed by the pedagogical staff, its origins are quite different. The girl sees her stack of clothes, which is comprehensible to her, in relation to all that appears to her incomprehensible and thus hostile. Disorder of every sort is hostile, this begins with those objects that, precisely because they weren't stacked neatly in a cupboard, fall out at you when you open the door, but it ends in putrefaction, death and confusion, things the girl refuses to think about. She is able to withstand this onslaught of hostilities by arranging her stack of clothes in such a way that it remains comprehensible. It is more than her own tidiness she is preserving by these means, but of this no one, as yet, has even an inkling. And if one or the other pupil should be struck dead by the objects falling out at him from his locker, or else by one of the teaching staff after discovering this disorder during locker inspection, this will quite simply no longer be plausible as an expression of the destructive principle once the girl has succeeded in wresting some bit of territory, tiny as it may be, from the control of this destructive principle, hereby establishing the simultaneous existence of disorder and order. This simultaneousness robs the calamity—one whose very essence is that there's no escaping it, no escaping it as a matter of principle—of its ability to exist.

But precisely this: the fact that the girl has never once come to the attention of the teaching staff during locker inspection, has attracted the attention of her peers. Her roommates, investigating this matter, examined the inside of her locker. The first thing they discovered was that even in the middle of the week, when no inspections take place, the clothes in the girl's locker lie neatly stacked, as though she never touched her locker or used any of the things contained in it, though of course she did have to get dressed every day and take out and replace certain school items. Secondly, the locker contains nothing more and nothing less than it did on her first day at the Home, nothing has been added which might allow the others to infer some human sentiment in the girl. The locker's metal doors are as bare as ever, not a sticker, not a photo, not a poster adorns them, though the Home's administration allows the decoration of locker doors—nothing, nothing, nothing. To the three others, it seemed practically inhuman that the girl's life should have left no traces where it was being spent. There must be a hiding place, they thought, and started rummaging through everything, but there was no hiding place.

During recess the next day, a few of the girl's classmates grab hold of her and the boy with greasy hair who had to repeat a grade, the class reject, and lead the two of them off to a distant corner of the schoolyard, beneath the chestnut trees, out of the range of vision of the teacher on duty. There they place a bicycle lock, stiff as the jaws of a trap, around both of their necks and lock them together. They had to make the girl bend over a little, for she is too tall even for this sort of jest. Then they run off. The girl and the boy with greasy hair have to stand there listening as the dry leaves of the chestnut trees tumble to the ground.

The weight of my life is increasing. Above me I erect a splendid palace. My palace is made of straw. It stands upon a hen's foot, I slaughtered the hen myself. When it storms, you can still hear its shrieks. I ornament my palace. It will make a beautiful bonfire.

The girl knows that her body is a transgression, she would like to atone for it, and so she obeys the decrees issued by her classmates to the letter. Thus she willingly stands with her eyes closed in the middle of the sports field, waiting for the others to hide and then call to her. But then they do not call, and not just for a quarter of an hour, but for many hours on end, at first because they have permitted themselves a joke at her expense, and later out of sheer forgetfulness, but the girl remains standing there all these many hours, first while the joke is being had at her expense, and later when she has simply been forgotten, for she stubbornly refuses to violate a decree, even after she herself has had to realize that it is only a joke being played on her, indeed the very decree itself was a joke, and even when it dawns on her with a probability bordering on certainty that sheer forgetfulness is to blame for this decree's not having been revoked. And when she observes that she will catch cold if she remains standing there for even a little while longer, she nevertheless refuses to violate the decree.

And so she remained standing in the place assigned to her and did not stir from it and thus she caught a cold. And at dusk a staff member found her still standing there and shouted at her whether she had lost her wits to be standing there like that and led her away. Don't you want to be able to have children some day? the teacher shouted, and with all his shouting failed to hear that the girl had quietly responded: No.

After this, the girl is sent to the infirmary to drink herb tea for a few days, take steam baths, and warm up again. The girl is happy. The infirmary asks nothing but repose for and of its patients, and for the sake of this repose, beds have been provided, freshly made beds with oversized pillows in which you can bury yourself. The girl doesn't have to move, indeed she is not allowed to, movement of any kind is forbidden. She is allowed to sleep, indeed required to sleep, as much as she can, and sleeping is one of the few areas in which the girl has achieved a high level of proficiency. All the rules that previously applied have now been suspended for as long as she lies here in her infirmary bed and is allowed, indeed required to sleep. There is no place from which the world appears farther removed than from an infirmary room such as this one. It is a place where one is sheltered, and what one is being sheltered from is, of course, the world, what else. One lies beneath the eiderdown and everything loud, everything pointy or bright, everything that might possibly beset one is repelled by this soft bulwark. To be sure, there are intrusions, in the form of measuring instruments, for example the thermometer, which is cold, but it would never cross the girl's mind to refuse them entry. When her temperature is taken, for example, she learns that it is precisely 39.2 degrees Celsius, and so her body loses a little of its monstrous incomprehensibility. This, too, makes it agreeable to be confined to the infirmary, for here there is a staff that is familiar with the mechanics of the human body. This body that might appear to its owner like a mound of flesh living its own life in a disorderly, even malevolent way, with no sense of why in the first place, or from where, or for how much longer, this body whose whims one is at the mercy of, which hurts, catches cold or gets infections, which begins to smell bad if not regularly washed and whose weight, even when it happens not to have a cold or an infection, nor to smell bad, is a burden one must bear without understanding it—this very body is here receiving the appropriate treatment as a matter of course. With relief, the girl thus recognizes that she must have more or less the same body as everyone else, leaving aside its lack of beauty, which is merely external. On the inside, then, her body is nothing out of the ordinary, and the illnesses that assail it are nothing out of the ordinary, and here one finds these specialists who know the girl's body just as well as all other bodies and administer to it just the same appropriate treatment as to all the others, because it is always one and the same mechanism. They ask only those questions which they ask always of everyone, and shortly thereafter they issue instructions that are just the same as they would issue in any other case and prescribe just what they would prescribe in any other such case under similar circumstances, and ask nothing not directly pertinent to the illness at hand. What concerns them is this machine, which is always the same: the heart, which is located in the upper left quadrant in every individual, or the lymph nodes, which are always to be found beneath the ears. This is what interests them. But what sort of figure one presents during the examination, whether one is huge, rough or even hideous, whether one is stupid or extremely stupid, all these things do not interest them, particularly not when all the signs are pointing unambiguously to a head cold. This happy staff, these happy specialists, they alone are able to relieve a living creature, at least briefly, of the great responsibility of having always to sustain this life that has been given one, always with only oneself to rely on, and without even knowing to what end. They say: Take a steam bath once a day, or: Take two of these tablets three times a day, or: Stay in bed, or: Drink only this herb tea and do not eat anything for the time being. And you don't have to lose any thought over the matter, let alone come up with the idea yourself that it would be best to take a steam bath once a day, or two of these tablets thrice daily, or stay in bed or drink herb tea and not eat anything for the time being. All you have to do is lie there, following the instructions of these people for whom life is a machine, and sleep a great deal. You can give yourself up to them entirely and, for once, turn your back on life.

The staff open the door to the girl's infirmary room without knocking, they pull back the sheets, various procedures are carried out, the girl's body is probed without anyone asking permission, measurements are taken and developments monitored, and the girl doesn't have to feel ashamed, for once she is permitted a furlough from shame, because it would make no sense at all to feel ashamed for having the same mechanism inside her as everyone else, she can be certain that no one here takes the least interest in whether or not she feels shame, what with her dark body itself lying spread out, open for inspection before the eyes of the specialists.

And so the girl rests in peace, she dozes or else sleeps, moving as little as possible, and warms herself beneath the heavy bedclothes. She is beginning to smell nice. The smell of her shapeless body vanishes almost completely, and in its place the aromas of health arrive, the smell of herb tea, the smell of the starched bedclothes and above all the smell of the disinfectants whose frequent use is the ambition of every hospital worker. The girl wallows in well-being as she thinks of the tiny parasites that inhabit her as they do every other person, parasites who now are in for it: these incarnations of the most vulgar gluttony. Teeming, invisible filth that is now being driven off, driven off by corrosive, caustic, radical measures. The girl gulps down the tablets that have been prescribed to help her fight off her cold, and then there is nothing left for her to do but lie there in the knowledge that these inhabitants of her interior are now in for it. From time to time nurses appear who lead the girl out from beneath her eiderdown, but when they take her by the hand, it is only to bring her to have her steam bath, and this does the girl good, she sweats everything that is sick within her out of her body, everything that is dirty, indeed one might almost say she is sweating her body out of her body. And when she returns from the steam bath to her bed, she can see how the bedclothes have twisted into a corkscrew to release her, the bedclothes lie in a sort of whirlpool, a sort of maelstrom, yet nothing at all has happened.

Beneath the covers it is very warm, warmer than anywhere else. Outside the bedclothes, in the infirmary room, even in the hallway of the infirmary, it is still warmer than usual, that is, warmer than is usual for a public or private building. It is somewhat less warm in the other areas of the Home, the dormitories, washrooms, activity rooms and sports facilities and the corridors that link them, yet here, too, it is still fairly warm, warm enough for one to exist under humane conditions. Throughout the grounds of the Home, the temperature can be described even in winter as perfectly reasonable, while outside the fenced-in grounds, beneath this self-same sky but outside the fence, this is not the case, that is one of the few facts from the past the girl can still recall quite clearly. And a reasonable temperature is one of those things that contribute to one's survival. The girl is quick to feel a chill, even in summer she feels chilly more often than the others, although she carries around much more fat on her than they do, such that one might be inclined to assume her fat would keep her warm. And when the others are unwilling to believe her when she says she's freezing, she shows them her arms, on which the little hairs are standing straight up with the cold, and when they continue to gaze skeptically into her blushing face, the girl plays her trump, which is her ability to make her teeth chatter at any time, and this is the decisive proof.

So she's freezing, and she has to sneeze, unusually often she is subject to sneezing fits that arrive suddenly and without warning. Even when she isn't sneezing, a droplet can frequently be found hanging from her nose, indicating that she suffers from a chronic sniffle. Even in summer, in the middle of summer, when everyone else has forgotten there is such a thing as the sniffles, the girl has to curl into a ball at her desk to blow her nose. She curls up to blow her nose which had a droplet hanging from it, because she is ashamed, not only of having the sniffles, but also of the old, disintegrating scrap of tissue she is using as a handkerchief. Even her sniffles are sniffles on the lowermost rung of the hierarchy, unworthy sniffles that make the mucus flow out of her nose like an old lady's, not an ordinary cold such as makes people's noses stuffy for a week, forcing them to breathe through their mouths, and then it's over, no, nor is her sneezing ever a lovely, liberating explosion, rather it is practically feline, a stifled, spasmodic snuffling, as if it were a cat sneezing.

Even apart from this sniffling, the girl's health is quite fragile, in marked contrast to what her stature might lead one to expect. To be sure, you can tell at once that this girl is not an athlete, and that she therefore is not likely to number among those who are particularly hardy, but to how great an extent she is in fact susceptible to every sort of mundane and, as will later become clear, more serious illness is not immediately apparent when you first see her, the impression she makes is far too robust. Her form, which gives an initial impression of repleteness, leads one to infer solidity within. But as it turns out, just the opposite is true: The reason her body has swollen out of all proportion is that it is unable to utilize appropriately the substances provided it in great quantity thanks to the girl's voracious appetite. On closer inspection, it appears this body is simply accumulating without rhyme or reason all that has ever been introduced into it, as though misguided stinginess made it unwilling to surrender anything at all, as though the body itself were merely a great, blind cache, a stock-pile whose contents, however, cannot be put to use because the instructions are missing—the impression one has is of a ruinous mass, one that is alive, to be sure, for a body must necessarily be alive, but at the same time somehow dead.

And perhaps it simply isn't true that it is out of immoder-ateness that the girl must eat so much, as the others always claim with disgust, perhaps it is her only chance at survival. It isn't true that all this food allows her to survive much better than the others—she is barely surviving—it's just that she has to eat far more in comparison with the others in order to preserve at least some degree of life despite this difficult body of hers, which is lacking even the most fun-damental powers of resistance. For example, the girl has only to spend a quarter of an hour sitting in a draft, perhaps because the teacher is airing out the classroom, which, no one knows why, smells of rubber, and already she can count on her neck becoming stiff for the entire next week, her sniffle worsening, and her ears beginning to ache. And naturally this earache is no run-of-the-mill earache, of course not, it will invariably be accompanied by a whistling sound that only the girl can hear, inside her. The music teacher made her sing this sound for him, and he identified it as F-sharp two octaves above middle C.

Leaving aside the pain, which an illness brings to the girl just as it would to anyone else, time spent being sick is generally considered disagreeable because it is nothing but a waiting period, empty time. Children get bored to death and spit out the herb tea because they find its taste insipid, and when they are older, they will describe the experience as having been chained to their beds. Bed, however, and the notion of being practically chained to it, are things to which the girl has no objections whatever, bed is without a doubt the safest place in the world, and what is more, one of the warmest. Nonetheless, there is something unattractive about being sick, something embarrassing, and this is the interruption of quotidian existence which the illness brings about, the special status that someone who is frequently ill must necessarily acquire. Of this, the girl is ashamed. You might almost say that it is her shame over being sick so often, more often than the others, this fear of not appearing normal, this embarrassment that is the real torment, and you might almost assume it to be this embarrassment that makes the girl ill so often, a diabolical cycle. And all the while she is feeling the most intense longing for an infirmary bed. It would be conceivable that her frequent absences from school might lend her a certain standing among her fellow pupils, that she might begin to appear somehow anarchistic if the others assumed she was only playing truant in a particularly cunning way. This might cost her the lowermost rung in the hierarchy which has so miraculously come into her possession and which is, moreover, the safest one, possibly she would rise to a higher rank and then have to prove herself worthy of it, from then on she would be tested for her suitability, since every rank, every rank except the lowermost one, is defined by ability, not inability. The girl would be wrenched from the warm comfort of having been forgotten and would be forced to act. It might also be that through this excess of illness she might accidentally begin to arouse pity after all, that the others might begin to go easy on her, to stop pushing her down, and from this moment on the girl would be condemned to life as a foreign body, all her efforts to achieve normalcy through failure would be vanquished once the pity began. All these thoughts taken together cause such horror to erupt within the girl that it makes her ill, ill once more—her customary sniffles are joined by a fever which leads her by the most direct possible path to a bed in the infirmary. And there, ensconced once more in her infirmary bed, she is overcome by a feeling of the most immense, undisguised joy.

In this respect, then, the girl is defined by contradictions which she attempts to escape all the more urgently as soon as she is no longer ill. For example, she likes very much to join, dressed like all the others, washed like all the others, the group of pupils who pour out of the school building once classes have ended to go to the dining hall. And she succeeds in this, though all the others are walking in pairs or small groups, chattering among themselves, and she herself is walking alone since no one has any interest in talking to her, nonetheless she succeeds in leaving the build⁄ing as a part of this group, nonetheless she contributes her share to the throng and its odor, the throng and the odor of eighth⁄grade pupils on their way to the dining hall after school. This pale, huge creature sits down with the others at the food⁄stained table, at the eighth⁄grade table, among all her classmates, no one can object to that, and if someone does object to it, it will be at most a sort of mockery that is internal to the table, the eighth⁄grade table, a clarification of the table's internal coalitions, a negative sort of recogni⁄tion, but recognition nonetheless, perhaps she will even be received as a glutton with welcoming jeers. It may happen that someone spits in her food, but she doesn't have to sit alone, doesn't have to be a loner, doesn't have to be anything out of the ordinary. The others watch as she silently shovels the food into her mouth, on some days she even goes so far as to ask whether she may finish off the scraps remaining on their plates should something be left over, gnaw the bones, lick up the sauces, clean out the pudding bowls with her finger, suck the last flat drops from their drink cartons. Tormented by the most intense cravings, she is able, on lucky days, to come by these eighth-grade leftovers, she eats that of which the others have eaten, drinks that of which the others have drunk, this purifies her blood. Whereas generally she is colorless, nearly to the point of invisibility, the concentration she brings to the activity of eating gives her the appearance of having character. Thus while the girl arouses the displeasure and disgust of those before whose eyes she is eating so immoderately, she is nonetheless partaking in the general conviviality, and this displeasure and this disgust are quite ordinary displeasure and disgust, they are perfectly quotidian, the cruelty her classmates are particularly fond of doling out during mealtimes is a perfectly normal cruelty, one the girl can count on, it is cruelty to which she is entitled, and above all it is not nothing. Occasionally someone will bring up the bucket of pigs' eyes that had appeared beside the teacher's desk the morning a dissection was on the program in biology class.

The eyes had been distributed among the class so that each pupil really did have an eye of his own, and it was astonishing what exertion was needed to penetrate the tough outer membrane with a scalpel—when this had been achieved, the fluid from inside the pig's eye ran over their hands. The girl eats silently and with great appetite without once looking up from her plate, her thorough chewing motions punctuated by hiccups, stubborn uninhibited hiccups, such as only children get. At such moments it is quite possible that someone seated directly across the from the girl will feel the urgent need to rip the Band-Aid from the oozing fever blister on his upper lip and display to the girl this festering wound, asking whether she knows of a good cure for his malady. The girl is imperturbable, virtually bovine, she says she doesn't know of any cure and while speaking continues to chew her sausage, her vegetables, she gives the upper lip a cursory glance, but does not meet the gaze of the one who has asked her advice, the hiccups are still not under control, she chews, and she has placed both elbows protectively around her plate on which she has piled a quite respectable portion. Like an ox that has been hitched before a plow, she plods onward, says no, she doesn't know of any cure, and this answer is utterly unsullied, absolutely pure, for while it has already been demonstrated on many occasions that the others can be expected to treat her unkindly, that the others are incapable of being well-disposed toward her, she nonetheless shows herself again and again to be astonishingly proficient at forgetting this. Just as a puddle into which a stone has been thrown is able shortly afterward to entrust itself to gravity once more and form a level surface, the girl, too, possesses just such an earth-bound, unsulliable nature. Thus the jokes made at her expense must be particularly crude if they are to have an effect at all and not just pass by unnoticed. To the amazement and general amusement of all, on the other hand, it was discovered that pranks whose effectiveness has already been proven can be repeated over and over again absolutely unchanged without the girl's learning over time to parry them with greater skill. For example, the others once succeeded in taking away her plate of food during a meal by asking her to clap her hands. She didn't attempt to defend herself, just sat there and quietly began to cry. Never would it have occurred to her to leap from her seat and try to get her plate back, never would she have begun to fight, although her chances would surely have been quite good considering her size. Eventually she stopped crying. When the next day someone asked her to clap her hands while she was eating, she of course did so, and of course her plate was taken away from her once more, and so on. It is hardly conceivable that anyone could be so forgetful. While the others spend their lives amassing hidden thoughts and deriving logical consequences from the comparison of different events, the girl is honing her skills in the art of forgetting.

The less the girl speaks, the less she can do wrong. And, as eventually becomes clear, there are various ways in which she can succeed by her silence. Once during gym class the underpants that had just been allocated to her were stolen, the single pair of underpants that is hers for the week, and the weather is beginning to turn cold, the first snow has fallen. So all she had to put on was her skirt and her stockings, and now the wind can slip beneath her skirt unhindered, already it seems she is beginning to catch cold. The next day, the girl sees five boys from her class playing soccer with her underpants during recess. After this, there is no sign of them, but when another three days have passed she finds a note in her schoolbag with a drawing of her underpants and the words: You've swept all day, now put it away! It takes the girl three hours to decipher this message, then she calmly walks over to the dormitory building, climbs the two flights of stairs to the floor where her room is, and walks down the linoleum of the windowless corridor all the way to the end, to where the broom closet is. She opens the door to the broom closet, the smell of floor wax rises to greet her, and, lo: there are her underpants, stretched atop a broom standing upside down in the corner. The girl plucks her underpants from the broom and, right there in the closet, pulls them up under her skirt.

A few days later chance will have it that the girl surprises the five underpant thieves, appearing as if out of thin air upon the wooded hill behind the Home from which she can see everything, just as they have begun to work over a small

63

boy from the third grade. Four of the five are holding him down, and the fifth is kneeling above him and appears to be stuffing his mouth with dirt. Even before the five can release the smaller boy, the girl has already turned around and vanished. All week long the five boys are terrified of the girl, they avoid looking at her so as to keep their fear in check. Boys who attack a third-grader five against one fall without question into the category of juvenile delinquent, and delinquents are sent to an institution designed especially for their ilk, where life is far less pleasant than in the Home, that's what the five are afraid of. But nothing happens, the girl does not report what she has seen, despite the fact that she is clearly, for the moment, in a position of strength. She must be blind or else simply too stupid to commit even an act of revenge requiring so little effort, at least that's what the boys conclude in light of the mercy that has been shown them by their victim. From the girl's perspective, however, these two incidents—the theft of the underpants, and the free-for-all in the woods—do not appear to be related to one another. It is as if she is altogether lacking in self-interest. Each of the events exists for her in its own right, as if a bridge in her head—the one that in most cognizant beings links what has been done to them to what they do to others—has collapsed.

In any case the girl has a great deal of trouble deriving independent thoughts from something she has seen, this has often enough become apparent during various class sessions. And where it is a matter of thought becoming speech, that is, thought's pointing to something beyond itself, even being translated into action, such as is necessary for a betrayal, then there is little to be feared from her. In this particular case there is the additional complication that in order to carry out this betrayal the girl would have to go to the teachers' lounge, the designated location for communicating such complaints—and for her, entering the teachers' lounge is something that lies beyond the realm of possibility, even if she wanted to she wouldn't manage it, for the teachers' lounge lies at the far end of the ground floor corridor, and this corridor approaches infinity, at least that's how it appears to the girl. The teachers' lounge is beyond her reach, just looking down the corridor makes her dizzy. She stands at her end of the corridor like a fish behind the glass wall of an aquarium—the fish, too, is simply unable to swim through the glass, it, too, has no alternative but to remain silent, and thus if you know the girl it is in no way surprising that she didn't talk, didn't recognize her advantage when it presented itself or at the very least didn't make use of it. It is thanks to her that the machinations of her classmates remain hidden from sight.

The week after she, who knows why, didn't say anything, kept her mouth shut, as her schoolmates say with already something verging on respect, one of the boys from the fifth-grade corridor comes flying across the courtyard, pursued by a teacher. The girl is just taking a scrap of something from her pocket to blow her nose when the one being pursued stumbles over her in full gallop while glancing back at his pursuer. But instead of cursing and giving the girl an additional kick as might ordinarily happen, he simply gets up without a word, and in a desperately foolhardy impulse presses money into the girl's moist hand, the stolen money, apparently, because of which he is being pursued. Hastily he whispers something to the girl and then dashes off. The girl is holding the money in one hand, her ragged handkerchief in the other, and her nose is running. She follows the boy with her eyes for a moment, then looks in the other direction to where the teacher, having just abandoned his pursuit of the boy for want of strength, gazes after the miscreant in exhaustion. The teacher does not see the girl, even though she is in his line of sight, he looks right through her to where the fugitive is standing, and even if he saw her, it would never occur to him that this creature might have anything whatever to do with the troublemaker's plot. Now the girl doesn't know whose money she is holding in her hand, whether it is the teacher's or that of a fellow student. What the boy on the run whispered to her was: Hold on to this! And so the girl, without a thought, puts the money in her pants pocket, she neither wonders anything nor does she speak, she simply puts this money, which doesn't interest her, in her pocket, then finally blows her nose using both hands and afterward stuffs the handkerchief on top of the money. And at just this moment she remembers something, remembers something for the first time. She remembers that the name of the boy who has just whispered to her is Björn.

This very day at dusk, the money thief named Björn takes a stroll over to the playground where the girl spends evening after evening perched in solitude upon a metal bar, motionless as a hen that has already tucked its beak beneath its wing for the night. But when Björn walks up to her and holds out his hand, the hen begins to stir, without getting down from the bar she reaches into her pocket and retrieves, in turn, first the handkerchief and then the money, the latter she hands over to her classmate while returning the handkerchief to its place. He counts the money, none of it is missing.

Thus it has been demonstrated: the girl can be put to use. From this moment on, the girl senses a shifting of the fronts, a sort of collective change in the direction of the wind, the cause of which remains obscure to her. The sensation is agreeable. Instinctively she tries to do everything just the way she did on this day when, for the first time ever, a classmate whispered something to her. Blind and happy, she stands here with this warm breeze wafting over her and doesn't want to move ever again. She refuses to surrender the sweater she wore this week to the laundry collection, she won't let them cut her hair—the important thing is that along with the various other habits she unnecessarily retains, she also continues her habit of not speaking. She settles into silence without realizing that her silence is the first thing about her that her classmates have ever prized.

When the girl first entered the Home, it felt to her as if she were attempting to dive into a body of water. She never perceived a single face in isolation, but rather only a flood of faces, and she rowed. Now that she has apparently succeeded in diving beneath the surface in a modest, quiet way, now that she is being allowed to swim with the current, she begins to encounter various distinct individuals. From this moment on, this moment when she is able to hold in her memory the knowledge that one of her classmates is named Björn, she begins to retain other stories as

well. Her head ceases to be empty, it is now a head containing the stories of a fourteen-year-old girl.

The first thing she notices are the ink-stained hands of the
boy who sits next to her, the one with the rough-hewn face.
And once she has compared these hands, not without a
certain shame, to her own hands, which are pale and free of
stains, her eyes wander up to the rough-hewn face. The boy,
no doubt hoping to contain a nosebleed, has stuffed a plug
of paper into his right nostril. Then the girl unexpectedly
remembers that once, in physics class, this boy constructed
an astonishing electrical contraption, a contraption that,
when you pushed a button, made countless little lamps light
up. As if she has only now attained the peace of mind to
cobble together these fragments, the girl finds herself unexpectedly able to understand various things that had
heretofore bewildered her. She observes her neighbor with
the plug in his nose, twisting her head up to peer at him
without, however, ceasing to keep it hunched between her
shoulders, and recognizes him as a being possessed of
unusual powers of invention and technical insight. The

ink-stained hands and the plug are just as much a part of this person as is the astonishing electrical contraption, at any rate they suggest that for this particular person other things are more important than a well-groomed appearance. This person is named Erik. Suddenly she knows the name of her neighbor beside whom she has sat for three entire months without once daring to look at him, let alone remember him, and she will no longer forget the names of the others, either. The girls with whom she shares a room are named Mandy, Nicole and Babette. Many in the Home have names like this, suggesting that names were the only things that could be had for no money when they came into this world. Mandy is tiny, like a dwarf, Nicole has blond hair, and Babette has a cross hanging around her neck and secretly says the Lord's Prayer before she goes to bed.

It has grown cold, the asphalt roads of the Home are covered with watery snow, the sky is full of sulfur, and an icy wind is tearing the last rotten leaves from the poplars along the avenue, crossing the grounds in a straight line without curves of any sort, as if to illustrate the idea of discipline. For the girl, this is the beginning of the Golden Age.

The girl learns to play skat. The young people sit in the classroom, the teacher speaks, and the young people play skat. This skat game takes place between several rows of desks, with the pupils seated in the rows closest to the front half-turning their heads toward the back of the room, they glance over their shoulders at the discard pile and non-chalantly add cards of their own. The game is pursued heartlessly, boldly, indifferently, depending on which teacher is fighting his lonesome battle at the front of the room with the help of a greater or lesser degree of violence. Eighteen!, Twenty!, the pupils hiss under their breaths, while, for example, a slimy, worn-out voice is going on about the quantities of crude oil found in the region around Baku. The teacher can pull his pupils' hair if he thinks he will achieve something in this way, but he will achieve nothing at all.

The young people are blowing notes to one another containing things that could just as well be discussed during recess, in the opinion of the teacher with bleached-blond hair, but in this she is mistaken. Now that the girl's vision is sharper and she is less frightened, she can see these notes flying about, see what invisible lines are being stretched across the classroom, and she begins to speculate as to the contents of these epistles. She waits for the faint explosive sound that accompanies the launch of one of these conspiratorial little balls of paper, and joins the others in giggling over the teacher's impotence to stop these projectiles. For the first time in all her months here, she can be seen giggling with all her heart. Her neighbor Erik is already at work on a catapult for these wadded-up communications, though he is also in possession of a mechanical pencil whose tube might be used to propel this airborne mail. He has already made a sketch of the catapult, and now it is only a matter of completing its construction while the teacher is transferring a complicated diagram onto the blackboard with her back to the students. A few of them are laughing at the teacher's all too short leather skirt, from which two alarmingly bowed legs protrude. The topic of the lesson is subject and predicate. The teacher is marking everything she wishes to have recognized as a subject with a double underline. Her hands are finely powdered with chalkdust, and beneath the chalkdust her skin is splitting.

The contact between the girl and the others becomes closer over the course of the winter, even though it has nothing to do with shared tastes and aversions, or with any commonality of cowardice or courage, rather it can be likened to the intimacy between a man and the factotum who delivers his messages, between a conspirator and the guards posted before his door, between a mistress and her maidservant. The girl begins to do things that might lead one to suspect that her devotion to her classmates borders on idiocy. For example, she makes use of the time allotted to the pupils during a test to copy out the correct answers in a tidy hand for her classmates and surreptitiously pass them to the interested parties. What is surprising is that the girl is suddenly, who knows how, more and more often in possession of the correct answers, and surprising, too, is her ability, only now become apparent, to mimic the handwriting of others well enough to deceive. It remains a mystery, on the other hand, why she displays no interest at all in turning in the correct answers herself.

The girl appears to be content in her mute devotion to her classmates, and when these classmates wage war among themselves, she can reliably be found standing, unencumbered by any opinion of her own, on the side of those who have found a way to use her for their purposes, and when both sides find a way to use her, she is on both sides at once. Since all that is required of her is to hold on to what has been entrusted to her, or say what she has been asked to learn by heart, this is perfectly feasible. The place she occupies in the classroom hostilities is therefore not always an honorable one, it isn't really a place for a human being at all, since it forces one to approach zero, all one's insides must be emptied out like a fish before frying, and only then will there be sufficient space for storing the misdeeds of others, others' happiness and others' grief. But the girl already had such a space within her when she arrived at the Home, she has the heart of a maidservant, and fortune has decreed that she should now find employment among her classmates.

While not long ago the girl herself fell into the cesspool because she was chasing after the others and failed to notice the flimsy board that had been laid across the pit and camouflaged with foliage, she is now one of those who lure new pupils across this board. And then she laughs, opens her mouth up wide to show her teeth and laughs sound‐lessly but with all her heart.

Now she can be seen trotting across the grounds like a horse, bearing a smaller child on her shoulders, the way one of the older pupils might give a younger sibling a piggy‐back ride. She is seen running about the dormitory building of the lower school in costume, clutching the top of her head with both hands to keep her crown of feathers—which doesn't quite fit—from falling off, behind her a throng of whooping Indians. She is seen playing hopscotch with the younger children although her feet are so large they barely fit between the lines that have been scraped out in the snow. Her classmates have initiated her into the family structures they have invented for themselves. Each of them has a little brother or sister in one of the lower grades for whom he is responsible. The younger child is subordinate to the older one and must obey him, but in return the older one protects him from the teachers and staff, retaliates for wrongs done to him, takes revenge. But the girl has somehow misunderstood this system, she seems not to have fully understood that its structure is hierarchical, for instead of finding herself a little brother or sister to be her subordinate, she begins to play with the younger pupils, not impatiently or with intent to instruct, the way older pupils generally play with younger ones, but wordlessly and with abandon, as among equals. During recess she goes sliding with the little ones down the slope the first hard frost has coated with ice while her classmates stand in two corners of the schoolyard, furtively smoking. The girls stand in one corner, in the other the boys. From both corners, their incredulous glances follow the girl as she slides down the icy slope with the younger children, but they speak of more important things. After school, too, the girl can be seen sliding once more, like a scarecrow, her arms held wide to help her keep her balance. Until nightfall she remains, and in the end she is completely alone, as the time for the little ones' supper has passed.

There had always been jokes of a certain sort concerning the girl, jokes having to do with her size and bulk which were therefore never quite innocent. For while the girl did not have large breasts, such as would have been fitting for such a body, but rather just two modest little peaks, there was a certain wobble there, a definite flaccidity, and this had sufficed to arouse the fourteen-year-old boys. They themselves were unable to understand what it was that had abruptly caused their revulsion to give way to lust, filling them with the urge to get rough with her. But now that the girl has for the most part fallen silent, now that it has become clear how completely one can rely on her mental neutrality, her physical neutrality is beginning to manifest itself, and the provocativeness once displayed by this wobbling, uncoordinated yet at the same time reticent piece of flesh appears to have vanished. This body, it appears, is not provocative at all, and there would be little point getting rough with it, as it is sure to offer no resistance whatever, and so any lust directed toward it—lust tempered with aversion, to be sure—will sink into it as if it were made of felt, it will simply be swallowed up, absorbed, suffocated. In retrospect, the boys find their earlier attacks on the girl's skirt and underpants incomprehensible. This creature, which at first, though unclean, oversized and coarse, was clearly female, now becomes someone in whose presence the circles of both male and female intimates alike do not hesitate to speak without shyness or even premeditation about sexual matters. They begin to entrust the girl with notes that she is to deliver to this or that fellow pupil, and unfailingly she returns with the answer, they teach her special combinations of knocks by which she is to warn them when a teacher is approaching, then they station her in front of a dormitory room, whose door they barricade from the inside using a mop handle. The first time she stood watch like this, she was frightened out of her wits when someone inside the room began to whimper and moan as though he were dying, but the girl stuck to her post, and meanwhile she has gotten used to these noises and no longer wonders about what sort of pain this is.

Whereas there almost never used to be a seat free when the girl wanted to do her homework in the common room—usually she had to sit on the floor with her notebook, which she endured without complaint—now there is room for her, she is tolerated by the others, and now and then someone even asks her a question. The girl always answers either Yes or No. Questions that cannot be answered with Yes or No she simply leaves unanswered, she pretends she has to think about the answer, and then continues to think about it until her interlocutor has forgotten the question. The girl develops a special technique that allows her, even when she is answering only Yes or No, to make her answer as small as possible so as not to cause embarrassment for anyone by her agreement or disagreement, she bends down under the table as if to retrieve some fallen object while saying Yes or saying No, or else she hides her face behind her fists and murmurs into them. She herself asks no questions, not only out of shame, but also because she wouldn't know what questions to ask.

What do you want to be?

The girl is silent.

I don't know what I want to be yet, maybe a veterinarian. But there's still time.

Silence.

The girl sits there in silence, she doesn't bend down under the table as if to retrieve something, she doesn't hide her face behind fists, she just sits there in silence. And while Nancy is going on about the poor whales, the poor lions and the poor rats, the girl's nose begins to run, and it seems to her as if she has lost, along with her memory of what used to be, her memory of what is supposed to be some day. She appears to herself like someone who has been charred into a little ball, someone who has been charred in time as in a fire and is now nothing more than a blackened lump that has been deposited at a home for children.

The girl is very grateful, and though she doesn't speak much in general, she does say Thank you rather frequently, indeed sometimes does so even at moments when others might register complaints or at least voice disagreement. For instance, she says Thank you when one of her classmates, Maik, a lanky boy with a face like a bird, takes her best ballpoint pen away from her with a curt nod, so he can weight his paper airplanes with it. Once, in the middle of a turbulent physics lesson, this Maik had his face slapped by Saskia, a hirsute dark beauty who had been hoping by this act to create a stir—in which she did not succeed. Maik, however, succeeded in this, by slapping Saskia right back, whereupon she began to bawl, and the red spot burning on her left cheek was still visible at recess. It is this story the girl is thinking of when she thanks Maik for taking her best pen away from her. She is saying Thank you for the privilege of knowing him.

The girl's dreams are coming true. It began when Babette, her devout roommate, gave her one of her bracelets, one of those colorful woven bracelets children like to wear. And the girl is no longer excluded when the others make plans in her presence to watch television in the evening or have tea together in the afternoon, they are permitted to make tea in the little kitchen next to the TV room. Often the girl has shown up for these dates and, according to plan, is allowed to take her place beside the others on the threadbare couches in the TV room. Sometimes, though, a date was set, and no one but the girl showed up. They had canceled the gathering without letting her know. Little by little she came to understand that these appointments were made of flimsy stuff, they either took place or they didn't, or they took place tomorrow, or the day thereafter, and word of the cancellation drifted about like a feather. Only because her longing was so cast in stone, her anticipatory pleasure so leaden, had she remained deaf to this light, childish variant of indifference. Little by little it dawned on her that there was no need to feel slighted, these occasions did not go to waste, and childhood was a thing bobbing upon a vast ocean of time. And so if on a Saturday afternoon her roommates should happen to leave the room without saying a word to her in parting, as if the girl did not exist for them, this is in fact the most veritable proof that they accept the girl as one of them. It means that the girl is now as natural a part of the inventory as their lockers and beds. When they start their day in the morning without a word of greeting, this means that there are still many many days lying before them, each indistinguishable from the next, and the faces they will encounter in the morning will be just the same for a very long time, so that it isn't worth making too much of them. One of these faces is the face of the girl.

In the evening, when the girl is already lying in bed with the blanket up to her chin, it now happens from time to time that one of the girls with whom she shares the room comes to sit on the edge of her bed and begins to speak in a low voice. The girl lies on her back with her eyes open, listening. One time it is Nicole, who for reasons beyond her comprehension is hated by the teachers—but that is not what is troubling her, what is troubling her is that she is in love with the mathematics teacher, whom first of all it is forbidden to love, and who secondly is so indifferent to her that of all the teachers he is the only one who doesn't hate her. Another time it is Mandy, the little one, Mandy who is almost as small as a dwarf, for some reason she can't grow any more, but that is not what is troubling her, what is troubling her is that she wants to go home, even though she hadn't even known what a potato was before she arrived at the Home, her mother had never given her a potato to eat. The girl is lying on her back, she has all the time in the world, it would appear, her eyes are open, and all the girls who wish to confide in her can be certain that she will never fall asleep while they are enumerating their woes, nor reveal anything of what she has heard, and from the point of view of those pouring their hearts out, this is highly estimable, comradely behavior. The girl's behavior might remind one a little of the way she stuffs herself with large quantities of food, for here, too, one can behold a silent gluttony which takes in everything, never to release it again, but this similarity does not occur to the others, perhaps because, while they are speaking to the girl, they always turn their backs to her. All these stories tumble down into the girl's cloudy head as if falling down a well, and there they rest.

Among real girlfriends it often happens that one who has let herself go in the presence of the other feels remorse for having told something that would have better been left untold, and now she feels she has sullied herself somehow.

For once you have said something that should have been left unsaid, even if only to a girlfriend, you have shouted it out into the world, and even if this girlfriend happens not to pass on the story to anyone else, it still has been shouted into the world, and of course you feel ashamed at not having been able to restrain yourself. But speaking to the girl about these things is a quite different matter. Telling her something isn't like shouting it into the world, it's more like thinking aloud. The girl lets the one who is speaking to her have the entire conversation to herself, she doesn't interrupt, doesn't interject comments of her own, doesn't seize control of the conversation, doesn't use what the other girl has told her as a stirrup to hoist herself into some story of her own, for she has no stories of her own. It is a pure seeing, a disinterested pleasure with which the girl receives these reports, and this explains the other girls' sense that they haven't divulged their secrets to anyone at all when they tell them to her. The girl simply lies there on her back, stringing monologues onto the iron bands that are wrapped around her heart. The others speak, and after a little while the thicket of problems that have been put into words begins to clear and the bit of advice the girl has not given them appears on the horizon of its own accord.

As these nocturnal sessions were just beginning, Nicole in particular, the blond one, worried that it might offend the girl to be spoken to of love, since she herself surely had no hope at all of ever being loved. Of course Nicole herself has just as little hope of ever touching the heart of the mathematics teacher, but this is a fanciful sort of hopelessness, the sort of pain suffered by a girl who is beautiful, a beautiful pain, a blond pain. She has no way of knowing that the girl not only feels no envy, but on the contrary feels that her very existence virtually depends on her ability to keep all contamination of this sort far from her own person, that it is only her own innocence that gives her sojourn here a meaning. Sometimes though, on quite rare occasions, the girl finds herself assailed by knowledge for seconds at a time while her girlfriends, seated on the edge of her bed, are making their confessions before her, it is as if the curtain the girl had sewn shut before her were suddenly being ripped open. At such moments she can no longer close her eyes to the fact that her companions are just in the process of leaving childhood behind them. Her own purity is the only thing that will be able to postpone its decay a short while longer, in this she trusts with the blindness of hope and grants them absolution.

The girl falls down. Early one morning, just before eight, right as she has arrived in front of the school building with the other girls, she slips in a puddle of melted snow and falls down and scrapes her knees. Everyone saw it happen, a few of them laughed, but Nicole, the blond one, helped the girl get up, Nicole took her by one of her huge elbows and pulled her to her feet, found a Band-Aid and placed it on the girl's bloody knee. Like the ribbon of a secret order, this Band-Aid, now hidden beneath long pants, adorns the scraped knee of the girl, and thus corre-sponds to the many other Band-Aids that adorn many other scraped juvenile knees that are hidden beneath long pants. At night, under the covers with a flashlight, the girl care-fully examines her knee and the Band-Aid Nicole has placed over the wound. She isn't surprised at having fallen, for the blood of one who takes up residence in the flesh of a child becomes child's blood, and child's blood is always looking for a way to escape into the open. Children do, in fact, fall down.

After this fall, the girl ceases to menstruate, she is now rid of the unpleasant odor, the nausea and cramps. The longer she succeeded in suppressing the pain during these episodes of indisposition, the more reliably the moment would come when everything went white before her eyes and she had to be escorted by a classmate down to the basement, to the women's lounge, the only room in the orphanage that was always ice-cold. Once it was Nicole who accompanied her downstairs, and once the girl had lain down on the couch, she covered her up, sat down on a chair next to the couch and held her hand. After a while she plucked up courage to ask the girl what it felt like anyhow to have blood running out of you like that, in other words what it felt like to be a real woman. The girl was seized by a sudden fit of nausea and without meaning to she vomited right in Nicole's lap, and although it was only bile, her guilt appeared to her virtually irrevocable, and for the next three days she was unable to look Nicole in the eye.

On Saturdays when many of the others leave the grounds of the Home, whether to visit their parents or, if they are over fourteen years old, to amuse themselves in the city until 8:00 p.m., the girl stays where she is. She doesn't envy any of the ones who leave the grounds, for she knows just how things are on the outside: You stand on a street full of shops with an empty bucket and wait.

On these Saturdays, right after locker inspection, she goes into the day room to see if there is anyone with whom a game of "Aggravation" might be played. If there is no one with whom a game of "Aggravation" might be played, she sits down at one of the formica-topped tables and begins in the especially slow way peculiar to her to write or draw something, anything at all that occurs to her, on scraps of paper she finds lying about. Then she folds up these scraps, puts on her anorak, goes outside and ambles across the muddy grounds. She doesn't even glance at the porter's lodge, which is buzzing with activity since today is visiting day—not out of defiance, she simply forgets to look, she is lost in thought.

The longer she spends in the Home, the better acquainted she becomes with its grounds, and a consequence of this better acquaintance is that she is compelled to move across them more and more slowly if she is to take note of all the particular points with which she is acquainted and savor each one in passing. At first she had seen the back of the kitchen building as a single long wall, but some time later it occurs to her that this back wall has an indentation, a fair-sized niche containing the back entrance to the kitchen, and it is there, in this niche, that the milk delivery service deposits its crates, then the kitchen employees open the door from the inside and drag the crates into the kitchen. So whereas not long ago the girl was just walking along a fifteen-meter wall, she must now, if she is to do the wall justice, also pace the length of this indentation and consider it, she has to look to see whether the milk delivery has arrived, whether the crates are just being dragged into the kitchen, or whether it is snowing on the milk. These and other matters. Sometimes, when no one is watching, she even taps her way along this wall, just to make certain. At the beginning of her sojourn here, the hill that stands at the edge of the grounds appeared to her rather small, but now that she has climbed step by step up one side of it and down the other, she realizes that the hill is in fact possessed of a respectable height and that it is more difficult to climb than was at first apparent. Beads of sweat appeared on the girl's nose even before she reached the top. Now, whenever she walks past this hill, she will no longer be able to dismiss it as a hillock, precisely because she is better acquainted with it, and she will observe it with new eyes and require more time for this observation, she will make a reckoning of the considerable length of time it took her to climb this hill, even if all she is doing now is gazing at it. To be sure, she will climb this hill a few times more, but with ever greater hesitation, and eventually she will cease to climb it at all, and not only because of the unreasonable exertion implied in every act of climbing. The concentration alone is enough to sap her strength: concentrating on the phenomenon that beneath her feet the mountain is, as it were, beginning to grow, that it is practically swelling beneath her as the girl makes her way up its vault. Eventually she will begin merely to stand there for a while at the foot of the mountain, observing or, whenever possible, touching a handful of earth that has been piled up or a trace in the mud in which melted snow has collected, and she will find an entire landscape in this little heap of earth, this muddy furrow. Static observation of this sort is a worthy substitute, she finds, for the tiring walk.

Did you grow up on the moon? they used to ask her during gym class, for they found it beyond comprehension that the girl didn't know any of the rules for the various ball games commonly played by children, and so the teams with hopes of winning feared and shunned her. She was, however, still capable of jumping—little jumps, but still jumps all the same, awkward lunges to the right or left by which nothing was achieved, but they did give the impression that the girl was at least trying to participate in the game in some meaningful way. Meanwhile she has learned to keep the rules for basketball, volleyball and dodgeball in her head, but she now also knows that there are hundreds of possibilities for doing something wrong. This knowledge robs her movement of that slight bit of élan it had formerly possessed. A rigidness overcomes the girl, like a great fleshy block she stands there on the playing field between her smooth-skinned, agile classmates, she is afraid of the ball, and her ability to at least get out of its way is in constant decline. Then it happens, the ball flies directly into her arms which she is holding crossed over her chest, and before she even knows how this has occurred, she is clutching this terrifying ball, clutching it and clutching it as if rooted to the spot, and the others are shouting, and the girl listens to all these shouts crisscrossing back and forth beneath the roof of the gymnasium.

Now it is still dark outside when the wake-up call comes. The instructor on duty bangs on the door from the outside, and a moment later, on his way back down the corridor, he pulls it open a crack, reaches inside and turns on the neon lights. The girl's three roommates are tossing in their beds, their eyes still closed. The rules thrust themselves right in the middle of their dreams, and the first thought to follow upon the dream is, without fail, the thought of the test that day in school, every day there is a test, not a single day passes all winter long without there being a test on something or other, the moment you put a toe out of bed you're already in the jaws of the test. Their hearts full of reluctance, these nymphs arise, slip barefoot into their crushed slippers and shuffle out of the room and down the hall to the washroom, where they brush their white teeth. The girl envies them the matter-of-factness of their displeasure, these clearly defined battle lines, the absoluteness of their ill humor, these children's indisputable right to feel defiance.

The girl herself is already lying there with her eyes open long before the first bang on the door, she is already awake, lying there with the covers pulled up to her chin while the other three sleep on, she does not stir, she just watches. Her eyes have become used to the darkness, and thus she observes the three others as they lie in their beds. They lie there in disorder, the covers clamped between their legs, saliva running out of their open mouths onto their pillows, they have gotten lost in sleep, Mandy, the dwarf, is counting in her sleep, millions upon millions she counts, the two others are quiet, Nicole is sleeping with her eyes half open, but this is only a physical defect, the girl has confirmed this: one night she crept up to Nicole's bed and held her hand before Nicole's half-open eyes without anything happening. The cross that Babette wears on a leather cord around her neck is now imprinting itself on her throat, it is squeezed in between her throat and the pillow. None of the three sleepers knows that the time allotted for sleeping will soon be at an end, for they are still surrounded by dreams, but the girl knows that in just a moment there will be a bang on the door. It is much more awful to know this than it is to be torn from one's slumber by a bang on the door.

On the thirteenth of February, the city was fire-bombed for the first time, it was bombed once, and then, as people were just beginning to creep out of the air-raid cellars, a second time, it was bombed so hard that the river on which the city lies began to boil, and of the city itself nothing was left. Now that so many years have passed since the bombing, the city exists again, and there is a home for children in it, and all the children have been called to assembly because the director wishes to make a speech. It is afternoon, the children are seated in the dining hall, the tables today are covered with white cloths, upon each table stands a burning candle and a plate of cake, but the cake may not be eaten until the director has finished his speech. The girl sees the white-clad tables and the candles, but above all she sees the cake, and eagerly anticipates the end of the speech. She listens carefully to what the director is saying, so as not to miss the end of the speech, and she has her eye on the largest piece of cake. But then something happens that has never before happened: The girl loses her appetite, at precisely the point in the speech when the director is telling about the boiling river, and how the people who tried to leap into the river to escape the flames were boiled alive. Maik gives a whoop, and Björn rubs his stomach in imitation of a canni-bal, but the girl loses every last bit of appetite, carefully she gets up from the table and without a word, by pressing the palms of her hands together, asks those seated around her to move their chairs to let her through. She goes into the

97

kitchen, sits down on one of the stools and remains there, gazing at the enormous rump of one of the cooks who is leaning out through the hatch to hear the director's speech. She asks the back of the cook: Why is there a birthday party when the people were boiled alive? She asks hesitantly, but the cook heard her clearly, as though the question were made of different stuff than air and had brushed against her body. She turns around to face the girl, like someone waking up from a deep sleep, and says: You have to cele‑ brate what you cannot forget.

Some days the girl doesn't comb her hair and is very quiet, quieter even than usual, and so tired that she falls asleep in the middle of a lesson. The teachers do not notice because the girl props her head in her hands as though she were thinking, a technique she has learned from observing her classmates. On one such day, Nicole walked up to the girl during recess and asked if she were sad. She even tried to put her arm around the girl, but this was awkward because the girl's shoulders are so broad, and so she took her arm back down again. All the girl said was that she wanted to sleep, she was so tired, so very very tired. Nicole didn't believe her, she raised her index finger and said: You mustn't be sad! And since the girl never does anything she isn't allowed to, she at once began to smile.

There is a secret meeting place, a shed whose lock is broken. Only rarely does the custodian come to fetch something from this shed: rakes when leaves have fallen, snow shovels when there is snow. And when he has raked the leaves or shoveled the snow, he returns the tools to the shed and hangs the lock in its place as though it would lock, but it doesn't lock any more. Often the girl had wondered where her classmates disappeared to after school, she'd kept her eyes open during her slow circuits across the grounds, and only rarely encountered one of them. But recently her classmates have stopped making an effort to conceal their meeting place from the girl. Her taciturnity has caused her to increase in value, in other words, she isn't seen as a nuisance. When she pushes open the door to the shed, the others no longer even turn around. She is allowed to join them, to sit down at the edge of the circle of secret smokers of both sexes, and, when she gets cold, to leave again, with neither her arrival nor her departure prompting anyone to question her. Once Saskia even offers her a cigarette, but the girl refuses it. Grandmother, then why do you have such yellow teeth? Saskia shrieks, and leans far back so as to show off what a large bosom she has already. Her intention is not to insult the girl, and this the girl knows. She is used to being used, to being taken by the shoulders and spun around, bent over or having her knees pressed forward to demon- strate a dance step or a game or something else, she knows she is well suited to providing an occasion for laughter that is so loud that all eyes fall upon the one who is laughing, not on the laughter's object. It is in just such a way that Saskia makes her joke about the girl, without genuinely wishing to subject her to ridicule—rather, her objective is to attract the attention of the boy standing next to her. It is Maik with the bird face, the one with whom she recently traded slaps, he is the one who's supposed to laugh, but he doesn't laugh, just continues to smoke and blow out the smoke through his nostrils and follow it with his eyes as it vanishes in the semi-darkness between rakes and snow shovels. Saskia gazes up at him the way women gaze up at a man, but Maik continues to look straight in front of him, the way men look straight in front of them when a woman is gazing up at them. The grandmother with the yellow teeth is standing near the circle, just outside it, for the moment she has been forgotten again, and thus she feels at ease. Outside a storm is raging, but inside this shed there is no wind.

Once the girl came into the shed, the sun had already set, she just wanted to have a glance to see if there wasn't someone there, noiselessly she entered since it is her nature to enter noiselessly, and at once she realized that something was wrong. She stopped just inside the door, and stood there in the shadows peering into the back part of the shed, which was lit by the orange rays of a streetlamp that came through the row of tiny windows just under the roof. The two boys in the shed didn't notice the girl entering because she didn't make a sound. She remained standing there and saw the two boys, one of them lying on a stack of hardened cement sacks, the other squatting beside him. She hadn't been able to understand what was happening and therefore, out of curiosity, remained standing there. The one who was lying down has opened his pants, and a newspaper conceals his upper body. The one squatting next to him has taken the penis of his companion in his ink-stained hand and is rubbing it. At the same time, he is speaking, he has a speech impediment and speaks with a lisp. He lisps: It's Nicole, your Nicole, kiss me, Dennis, it's Nicole, your Nicole, I've been waiting so long for you. Both boys are breathing quickly, expelling their breath in white clouds, it is cold. The one who is squatting rubs his friend's penis harder. He lisps: Let me show you my breasts, Dennis, it's Nicole, your Nicole, touch me, touch me between my legs, I'm already all wet, Dennis, Dennis, I want you to put it in me, put it in me Dennis, put it in me. The boy lying down moans and clutches at his friend, the semen spurts out of his penis and rains down on the newspaper, the girl hears the pattering sound it makes and leaves the shed. She walks for a little down the avenue of poplars, then stops short, takes hold of one of the poplars, bends down to the edge of the road and vomits up everything she has inside her.

No pain, no gain, the gym teacher had said. Meanwhile the girl's weakness goes far beyond gym class. There is the exertion of bending down from one's chair to take a book out of one's book bag, or the impossibility of answering in a loud enough voice a question asked by someone standing twenty meters away. For a while—as once when everyone began chanting in unison to urge on a fight—it had even seemed to her that her voice had grown stronger. But now she has stopped trying to fool herself. She had confused her own voice with the voice of the group, had thought she was shouting at the top of her lungs, whereas in fact almost no sound at all had come from her open mouth. When she is sitting on her perch in the twilight, she can see from a distance how Maik, Björn and the others are playing soccer, how they run about shooting goals of their own free will until dark, while she herself has to be happy she still has the strength to hoist her body up to this bar on which she so likes to perch. Inwardly she is tormented by a sentence that someone she can no longer recall said to her a long, long time ago: Everything you build up with your hands you knock down again with your rear end. Perhaps this is the source of the difficulty she has moving at all. The girl used to be constantly looking around to the right and left to be sure of doing whatever the right thing was, but now that she can see more clearly and perceives the great variety of human beings moving all around her in a thousand different ways, she can no longer choose what is right, she no longer knows what the right thing is. Everything she does seems to her wrong even while she is doing it, so utterly wrong that she'd like to take it back again—never would she have wished to offer offense to anyone, but now she is forced to realize that there is virtually no action at all that is free of the possibility of causing offense. At the same time, this state of being prevented from acting cannot merely be described as a lack of independence, as is so often done by the girl's teachers with pedagogical intent, it is more like a paralysis. Even transforming a simple thought into action, such as, for example, wanting to lift one's hand, is becoming more and more impossible for the girl the longer she remains in the institution. If you lift your hand, you must, a moment before, have wanted to lift your hand, if you laugh, you must have wanted to laugh, if you say no or yes, you must have wanted to say no or yes, in other words every time you do something, you must have wanted, a moment earlier, to do what you are doing. The moment you do anything at all, your volition can be seen standing naked behind it, and this the girl finds so utterly embarrassing that she chooses to want nothing. She wants what all the others want, but there is no such thing. And the moment she realizes this, she realizes also that her strength is waning.

The snow has turned gray, turned black and melted, and now there are great puddles everywhere. Then the sun begins to shine. The girl sits down in the empty day room on the first warm Saturday, when all the others have gone off together on some weekend outing, and writes a letter, a short letter on a scrap of paper, she writes extremely slowly, as is her habit, one capital letter after the other, like a faucet dripping, each letter stands there in isolation, unconnected to its neighbors. The girl folds the paper and writes in large letters on the outside: TO ME. Then she gets up from the formica-topped table on which she has been writing and pulls on her anorak. She stuffs the letter inside the anorak, next to her heart, and goes out into the sunshine. She places one foot after the other. She strolls across the grounds to the animal cemetery Nancy has secretly established for the poor rats, the poor mice, the poor little birds, strolls to where the little wooden crosses are standing, crosses on which are scratched the fantastical names Nancy bestowed on these creatures in honor of their deaths. Next to the animal cemetery she mails her letter, she bends down and inserts it between the boards of an old fruit crate that stands rotting upside-down beside a grave marked with a brick. This grave is the final resting place of the pigeon Kamikaze. The girl knows the story. Flying at top speed, the pigeon crashed into the window of Nancy's room one morning, then dropped to the ground, its neck broken.

The letter falls into the phosphorescent semi-darkness, joining all the other letters addressed TO ME. These letters, if anyone were ever to find and unfold them, would be full of sand, and it would no longer be possible to read all the words without effort, they are faded and smeared because snow has so often fallen upon the crate, or else rain, some of them are in fact entirely bleached out and are no longer anything more than folded dirty-white sheets of paper. But no one finds these letters, no one unfolds them, and no one makes the effort to read them.

One of them says: BE NICE, OR ELSE YOU'LL BE STRUCK DEAD. BEST WISHES—YOUR MAMA.

Another one: NEVER GO OUT IN THE DARK AGAIN WITHOUT YOUR CAP, OR ELSE THE CROWS WILL PECK YOUR EYES OUT. BEST WISHES—YOUR MAMA. This letter contains a sketch in which one can see seven dark birds flying toward the viewer bearing umbrellas, the flock is so dense there is scarcely any room left for the sky between them. The sketch is subtitled: THE BRETHREN. But now this inscription is blurred, and the sketch itself has faded beyond recognition.

DON'T STICK YOUR HEAD SO FAR OUT THE WINDOW, OR ELSE IT MIGHT FALL OFF. BEST WISHES—YOUR MAMA is one of the better-preserved letters. This one, too, contains a sketch, one that shows someone putting his head through an open window, but the upper edge of the window frame is serrated like the blade of a knife, and there is an arrow leading straight down from it to the neck of the one who is sticking his head out. Beneath this sketch stand the words: I AM TOO CURIOUS.

Another letter consists only of a sketch. It shows a very fat person, whether man or woman is impossible to say, perhaps it is supposed to be a snowman, for the creature is made of three spheres piled one atop the other, though the row of buttons is missing, the carrot and broom. This person has been marked invalid with two long crisscrossing lines. Underneath is written: HUNGER AND THIRST. The figure itself can scarcely be recognized any longer, but the two lines crossing it out are perfectly clear, and the subtitle has run in the dampness but remains legible.

The letter the girl mailed today reads: AS FAR AS I'M CONCERNED, YOU ARE DEAD. BEST WISHES—YOUR MAMA. Here, as in all the other letters, not a single written character contains a curve: the D has not a belly but four corners, the S is not a snake but a lightning flash, and the O is an empty square. The letters look as if they have been carved in stone, but the weather will eat away at them, just as it has eaten away at the other scraps of paper.

Early the next morning the girl is lying in bed preparing herself for the moment when the bang on the door will come. Then the bang on the door comes. The girl wants to get up, but she cannot get up. Her legs seem to her as heavy as if they were frozen. Then she begins to cry. The three others come over to her bed, drowsy and barefoot, and ask what the matter is, but the girl cannot explain herself. So get up then! The girl can't. Nicole kneels down beside her bed and doesn't know what to say. She gazes into this large, blotchy face, mute now, that is turned toward her, and it is like looking at the surface of an unknown planet. She is afraid of this immobile mass, and at the same time ashamed of her fear. The girl has let her head sink back into the pillows and has stopped moving. The only thing about her that is in motion is her nose, which is running. Nicole pulls a tissue out of the sleeve of her nightgown and wipes the girl's nose clean. The girl thanks her.

Then they come for her. She is lifted onto a stretcher and transported to the infirmary where she'd had to spend so much time upon her arrival at the Home. Recently she had been healthier. Slower, but healthier. Now she has a six-bed room all to herself, for no one else would think of falling ill in the springtime. Early on, she has them lift her a few times into a wheelchair and then rides—shouting with pleasure, to everyone's surprise—up and down the corridor at great speed. Then she quiets down, stays in bed all day, and then another day, and then another, waiting for visitors. She thinks the others can't come to visit her because they have to prepare for the big chemistry project. The day of the chemistry project passes, and then another day, and then another, and no one comes. Cast out of time, the girl lies in her hospital bed, but the face presented by each of the weekdays remains distinct in her memory. She can still remember with meticulous precision the structure of each individual weekday, right on schedule she feels precisely those feelings which she felt on each of these days when she still went to school, and thus she maintains her connection to her young friends. Thank goodness there's a clock in her infirmary room, so she always knows what feeling is in order. Even if she cannot move, she still keeps an eye on this clock.

And so on Monday from eight o'clock until nine thirty-five she feels English, with a little break in the middle. Then there is a feeling for the recess period. From nine fifty-five until ten forty she feels chemistry, and afterward, from ten forty-five until eleven thirty, biology. Recess feeling. Finally, starting at eleven fifty, she is overtaken by the exhaustion that always came over her during gym class. At twelve thirty-five on the dot she heaves a sigh of relief, the way all children sigh in relief day after day when school lets out. You might think all these minutes, hours and days the girl experiences chained to her bed were new, unprecedented. But this isn't true, they aren't new, in fact they wouldn't even be there at all if they hadn't already existed, once, in the era of the girl's happiness. In this way, Tuesday doesn't follow a Monday, but rather derives all its force from the fact that it is a Tuesday, week after week always a Tuesday—recognizable by a certain succession of school subjects and recess breaks. Although it is physically impossible for the girl to return to the scene of her crime, memory teaches her to stutter.

After school, after the precisely timed sigh of relief, the girl generally falls asleep, for she had never been able to achieve absolute certainty regarding the face worn by time at the end of the school day, the face of free time, she doesn't know whether to be happy or tense or indifferent or filled with nausea if she wishes to resurrect it. This had been a time of a thousand faces, one that resisted every form of planning, varying according to the weather, homework assignments, the promise of amusements, and sometimes it simply remained a mystery and the girl wasn't even able to learn what was going on. For this reason she now—i.e., starting Mondays at twelve thirty-five, Tuesdays at one twenty-five, Wednesdays also at one twenty-five, Thursdays not until two thirty, and Fridays already at eleven thirty—has

nothing to hold on to. Therefore she spends this time sleeping. Her sleep is interrupted only for meals, which take
place at the same times as for the others on the outside: tea
and cake at three o'clock, dinner at six. Only in this way
can she make herself believe everything is holding its breath
and remains familiar to her. The girl doesn't look out the
window, before which the trees are gradually unfolding
their green. In her head it is snowing and snowing.

Once she wakes up at ten after eight on a Thursday, she's
slept through the beginning of the first period: the beginning of gym class. The others have already lined up,
perhaps they've even begun the day's first races. For one brief
moment, the girl's lame body is filled with warmth, the
warmth of terror at having overslept. She doesn't understand how she could have done this, since the patients in the
infirmary are woken at six. Every one of these winter
Thursdays had begun with gym class at dawn. The sun
would rise during their endurance run. Today, though, the
sun is refusing to rise. Something is wrong. When the nurse
comes in, bringing the tea for the night, the girl realizes that

she mistook the time of day. It isn't morning at all, it's evening. She has bumped up against time like a blind person, at this she has to weep. And the hand she always used to blow her nose with is as heavy as lead, she cannot lift it.

The girl dreads the arrival of the first weekend, for she has no collective feeling, one common to her and all the others, for how a weekend should proceed. On weekends the pupils were always scattered to the winds, the fourteen-year-olds were driven into the arms of their parents and various amusements, which the girl neither knew nor wished to know. She wouldn't have had any notion what to feel on these infinitely long two days if there hadn't at least been locker inspection. As a shipwrecked sailor clings to a tiny bit of wood that is floating in the vastness of the ocean, the girl holds fast to her memory of locker inspection. On Saturdays early in the afternoon is when this general ransacking and purging of items that had not, in the opinion of the instructor on duty, been suitably stacked, occurred, a ritual which as such does not interest the girl at the moment—the little "s", though, that's the main thing, the little "s" at the end of the word "Saturdays", modest as it is, this "s", it consoles her. This "s" stands for order and discipline, it signifies that one knows what to do and what not to do, and in general that one knows how things stand. This "s" is the short but splendid tail gracing all these days the girl has been able to preserve in her memory: Mondays, Tuesdays, Wednesdays, Thursdays, Fridays and Saturdays —it sheds light on the girl's logical fallacy: mistaking what was for what is.

But all the long Sunday she spends exiled to her bed, the girl feels she might starve to death. On Sunday, too, no one comes to visit her.

In the end, the girl stops waiting, she tells herself that it is perhaps even a good sign that none of these children is willing to view her massive, breathing cadaver. She believes she recognizes in the absence of her fellow pupils that same healthy indifference she had noticed before when they neglected to take leave of her or when an appointment had been cancelled, an indifference she had come to respect. What she doesn't know is that the indifference the others now display with regard to her is more thorough than originally intended. At first, for example, Nicole was definitely planning to drop by the infirmary, but each time she was about to, something or other would come up, until finally she had to admit to herself that she felt a certain aversion— quite a strong one, in fact—to the idea of visiting the girl. A large, long sigh of relief sweeps through the classroom when it is announced that the girl's absence is expected to last for quite some time. While others who fall ill or have to leave the Home remain a topic of conversation for days and weeks on end, while everyone wants to know whether, in the one case, they are in pain or have to be operated on, or in the other, where they have gone to and what the reason was for their departure, even if they were only temporary residents of the Home—the girl's whereabouts, by contrast, are never discussed. This silence is all the more remarkable as it seems poorly suited to the position the girl had formerly occupied. It is too great a silence. It speaks of an extraordinary, indelible wrong. But neither Maik with the bird face, nor Nicole, nor Erik, the neighbor with technical aptitude, not even Björn or Saskia—no one would be able to say what it is the girl has done to make everyone erase her with their silence. But within them blossoms a great, monstrous hope: that she might never return.

The doctors, in an unguarded moment, referred to the girl's body as a bag of bones, and this figure of speech pursues her into sleep, she is compelled again to dream: of elbows slipping out of place, and of a skull so heavy it slides down beneath the skin until it rests between her knees, of ulcerous wounds, exposed sinews that have grown twisted together so that it is necessary to take a knife and slice through them.

Not once since arriving at the Home for Children has the girl left its grounds. Nothing in the world could have moved her to walk out through the gate of her own free will, even for a moment, and she took part in none of the popular group outings or class trips. But now it has come to this, the doctors, *horribile dictu*, are at their wits' end. We've done all we can do, they say, having completed all the examinations that can be carried out in the infirmary of a children's home, and they decide to send the girl to the General Municipal Hospital for a more thorough evaluation. As the orderly is hoisting the girl from her bed to the litter, she says: Over my dead body! The orderly shrugs: Whatever you say.

In the Municipal Hospital, the girl is brought to the children's ward, but above and below, to the right and the left of the children's ward, lie the adults, breathing. And every afternoon between two and five are visiting hours, and the ward fills up with people from the city, it fills with mothers and fathers, with flowers and cake. Every day between two and five, the girl buries her face in her pillow.

Thanks to the strict diet, something happens that no one would have thought possible: the girl becomes thin. All over her body, the now superfluous skin begins to droop in folds, and her face takes shape in a monstrous way: It is becoming the face of an adult. The doctors in the children's ward are the first to notice. Shaking their heads in disbelief, they appear again and again at the girl's bedside, and soon even the doctors from other wards come to join the group of those whose scientific curiosity has gotten the better of them. They observe the progress of this development and discuss among themselves how such a monstrous transformation could be possible. It is as if the excitement and hubbub generated by the girl's case, along with the struggle to comprehend what in fact the girl is, are increasing at just the same rate at which the girl is becoming, from each day to the next, sleepier and sleepier, scarcely does she so much as open her eyes any longer to distinguish all the many lab-coated persons who again and again assemble at her bedside, scarcely does she listen any longer to the diagnostic murmurings when various theories regarding her illness are proposed, discussed and rejected in front of her, as if she were still nothing more than a child. Within a period of perhaps two weeks, this face that, rough or coarse as it may have been, was still once decidedly childish, appears to recede, and in its place the features of a woman emerge, as if the illness were an artist who at last had succeeded in releasing the form once imprisoned in the stone. As if out of a general consensus that there must be something inde-cent about so unnatural an aging process, the girl in the end is summarily rolled bed and all into a single room, far from the eyes of the children with whom she had been sharing a ward.

But the girl does not continue to age and turn gray prema-turely as happens with those children who are born old, whose illness is well-known and has been studied, rather she ceases to age after approximately two weeks, when she has come to resemble a woman of thirty. And just as every realization reaches us in a state of increasing acceleration, just as every insight comes crashing down like an avalanche, that is, at first nothing at all happens, but then, at who knows what point in time and for what reason, the realiza-tion begins, and eventually, once the necessary courage has been mustered to consider possible the impossible, it becomes a force that cannot be held back by anyone or anything any longer—it is in just such a way that the process of realizing who the girl really is unfolds. Whether it was that even when the girl was still lying in the children's ward one of the visitors from the city recognized her emerging face, or that the doctors examined the girl's bone substance the way one might count the rings of a tree and then passed on the results, and that the police then began to search for the girl's face among their missing persons reports and not, as before, when the girl had turned up with her bucket, among the files of missing children—perhaps several of these things occurred simultaneously. In any case what was previously perceived as a genuine existence now is seen to have been a calculated deception, a masquerade and nothing more. The girl, who is no longer a girl, has laid aside her costume, her own skin, and before everyone's eyes has put an end to this carnival performance, as if her childhood were nothing but a joke, as if it had been given her to stroll up and down in time as in a garden, and in this attitude, despite all the modesty the girl displayed as a child and now continues to display unchanged, there is something offensive, something arrogant, a certain contempt for the natural course of things, even a challenge to God. This feeling is shared among all the members of the lab-coated audience who witnessed this inexplicable masquerade, but no one speaks of it. It is with satisfaction, such as that with which one might receive a long-overdue offering, that it is reported how often the patient is now seen to weep, she weeps even when her eyes are closed, in sleep, her prank has flopped, her attempt to stop time in its tracks has failed.

On Wednesday the doctor escorts a gray-haired old lady into the hospital room. Through the bars over the windows, which have been flung wide open, the smell of lilac floats into the room. The old lady is exhausted. Shame is written all over her face. The doctor pushes her closer to the bed. Here we are, he says to the woman lying immobile in the bed, this is your mother. The mother is silent. Oh, are you my mother? says the woman who used to be the girl, and very slowly she opens her eyes. I don't remember you at all.

© Katharina Behling

'Oppressive, charming, scary …
Jenny Erpenbeck is the rising star
of the German literary scene'
Cosmopolitan